Judith Cook is a freelance journalist. In 1981, she was awarded the Margaret Rhondda Prize for services to the public through journalism in recognition of her work on pesticides. Her other books are *Directors' Theatre* (1974), *National Theatre* (1976), *Apprentices of Freedom* (1979), *Women in Shakespeare* (1980), *Shakespeare's Players* (1980) and *Portrait of a Poison* (with Chris Kaufman) (1982). She is currently writing a follow-up to *The Waste Remains*, which is her first crime novel.

Judith Cook

The Waste Remains

Pluto Press

London and Sydney

First published in 1984 by Pluto Press Limited,
The Works, 105a Torriano Avenue, London NW5 2RX
and Pluto Press Australia Limited, PO Box 199,
Leichhardt, New South Wales 2040, Australia

Text designed by Claudine Meissner
Cover designed by Clive Challis Gr.R.

Typeset by Wayside Graphics, Clevedon, Avon

Printed in Great Britain by St Edmundsbury Press,
Bury St Edmunds, Suffolk

British Library Cataloguing in Publication Data
Cook, Judith
    The waste remains. — (Pluto crime)
    I. Title
    823′.914[F]   PR6053.05/

ISBN 0-86104-778-8
ISBN 0-86104-779-6 (pbk)

For Dr Kit Ballentyne

1.

The sea was like glass as Eddie Hutchinson crunched along the shoreline, deciding whether or not the heavy mist would clear so that he could go out and fish. Behind him, the single row of houses that make up the hamlet of Shingle Street on the Suffolk coast looked as if they were abandoned. It was six o'clock on a Monday morning.

Looking towards the part of the shore where a spit of shingle ran out to sea, Eddie noticed what looked like a bale of material washing gently in and out with the incoming tide. He walked over to have a closer look, but even as he approached, an unpleasant suspicion stirred in him.

The body lay face down. It was a man of medium height, dressed in jeans and a woolly sweater, and wearing plimsolls. Taking a deep breath, Eddie turned it over. Although it had obviously not been in the water long, sea creatures had already been busy on the face and Eddie did not take a longer look. He hauled the body up beyond the high-tide line and then raced back to the houses, where he woke a neighbour who had a telephone, and called the local police.

It took half an hour for the police car, closely followed by an ambulance, to arrive. There was no longer a local bobby and the nearest police station was some twelve miles away. Chief Inspector John Latimer, annoyed at being called out so early, gazed morosely out of the car window as he drew up.

'God-forsaken place,' he muttered to his driver.

Shingle Street lies at the end of a one-way track, almost an island, cut off from the rest of the land by a river and marshes.

Eddie led the police and the ambulancemen down to where the body lay. Latimer went expertly through the man's pockets, finding nothing but a few sodden pound notes and a packet of cigarettes, until he looked inside the shirt pocket. There, in a neat, plastic, waterproof container, was a press card bearing the name Charles Spencer.

'Name mean anything?' he asked the driver.

'No, can't say it does. Hang on, though; yes, now I come to think of it . . . I think he's the newish chap they've taken on at the *Evening Bugle*. Yes, I'm pretty sure that's the name.'

Eddie was hovering around, holding his hat in his hand, a rampant curiosity fighting with a desire not to get involved any more than he could help.

'What do you reckon happened?' he asked Latimer.

'Don't know yet. Can't have been in the water long. Probably one of those idiot dinghy sailors who go out without life-jackets and then fall in and drown. They get picked out of the sea every year. We'll ask around and find out if anybody's found an empty dinghy washed up hereabouts.'

After thanking Eddie and telling him he would be required at any subsequent inquest, Latimer returned to Stembridge and saw the body duly delivered to the mortuary. He then rang the police doctor and asked him to come over.

The doctor, a dour and laconic man, groaned. He had, he said, decided to take the morning off and play golf.

'Sorry about that,' said Latimer, 'but we picked up a body this morning. On a beach at Shingle Street. I don't imagine it will come to much, I imagine the bloke fell in and drowned. Anyway you'd best come along and see what you think. I'm just going to try to confirm who he was and what he was doing.'

It was another hour before he could decently ring the editor of the *Bugle*. Yes, the editor confirmed, sounding shaken, Spencer was a reporter. He had been with the paper a couple of months. He was quiet, diligent and seemed ambitious. He had come down to East Anglia from a London suburban weekly paper in search of further experience. He lived on his own in a flat in Ipswich and had no particular girlfriend. His parents lived in South London some-where. No, so far as he knew, Spencer had no boat of his own, nor did he have any particular interest in sailing. If he had, then he had not made it known and had not taken part in any of the activities of the paper's own sailing club.

He would, he said, contact Spencer's parents. He was very concerned over the death of a member of staff. Any help the police might want he would be only too happy to give. Spencer had not been expected in that morning. He had been working all day Saturday, so his failure to turn up at the paper would not have been noticed until much later in the day.

There was little more that could be done until the police doctor had finished the post mortem. But Latimer did not expect this to provide any dramatic results, so he went off in search of a coffee. Towards the end of the morning, he was just leaving his office to buy the first edition of the evening paper, when he met the police doctor on his way in.

'His name's Charles Spencer,' Latimer told him. 'Twenty-four years old, a Londoner, been working down here six months; has one of those new little flats just outside Ipswich. No wife, no special girl . . .'

He repeated again to the doctor his own theory that Spencer had gone sailing without a life-jacket and, being entirely inexperienced, had fallen in and drowned.

The doctor listened impassively and then said:

'If he did go into the water from a boat, then he was helped.'

'What do you mean?'

'He was dead before he ever got near the water. There's not a sign of any water in his lungs.'

'Are you trying to tell me he was murdered?'

'I'm not saying anything yet. There's something very odd about this one. He seems to have died from some kind of massive collapse. There's no sign of suffocation. He hadn't been bashed on the head. There are no wounds of any kind. There does seem to be some strange contraction of the muscles.'

'Surely to God he wasn't poisoned and then thrown in the sea?' asked Latimer, visions of his peaceful day receding ever further.

'I honestly don't know. I'm going to have to send some of the organs away for further analysis.'

'How long do you reckon he's been dead?'

'Hard to say with the body having been in the water. But I'd hazard a guess that it was no longer than thirty-six hours, give or

3

take a bit. Possibly a little more. I would say he probably died some time Saturday evening and probably went in the sea fairly soon afterwards, before any rigor set in. But that's a rough estimate.'

Latimer thanked him and turned to go back inside his office.

'Oh, by the way,' called the doctor, 'there were some external marks on the body, but they don't help much. There were scratches on his ankles and on one forearm which makes it look as if he'd been through some undergrowth. In fact I removed what seems to be a small piece of bramble thorn from his left ankle.'

2.

In Stembridge library, Janet Simms was passing a dull morning, assessing the recent spate of damage to library books.

'Why, oh why, do these wretched people have to write their boring comments in biro all over the wretched books?'

Her colleague, Irene, grunted agreement. Monday was always a quiet day. By eleven o'clock the only signs of life had been a couple of pensioners whiling away the time over the newspapers and Mrs Fiona St John Bartle, hotfoot after the latest Barbara Cartland. 'So clean and *decent*, so *wholesome* and yet so thrilling,' she had cooed, as she took it away clutched to her crimplene bosom.

Janet had been at the library now for a year. An erratic marriage had finally split at the seams, leaving her with a certain amount of cynicism and three children, currently visiting her parents in London for half-term. 'They couldn't wait to get away from all this fresh air and seaside,' she told Irene, ruefully. 'Even now they will be taking in deep breaths of petrol-laden fumes and stuffing themselves with Colonel Macavity's schlock Hamburger Eaties, while thinking about how to waste their pocket money.'

She was small and rather plump and was what someone had described, to her eternal chagrin, as 'sensible looking'. She was considered to be highly intelligent, had a penchant for Elizabethan drama, and a sure intuition for things that were not right. That intuition had led, during a sojourn in a local authority office library some time previously, to several council officials finding themselves in court on charges of corruption, while Janet, her task of organising the library completed, had moved thankfully on.

The period since the breakup of her marriage had produced no firm relationships. Men had come and gone in her life, valuing her common sense and stability but drawn by other, more exciting possibilities. The last of them had said all the usual things about not getting emotionally involved and she had laughed and agreed with him; but as she already had, she quietly took up her aunt's offer of her cottage on a cheap rental, found herself another job, and moved.

'Here,' said Irene suddenly, 'you knew Charlie Spencer, didn't you? He was quite a friend – kept popping in.'

'What do you mean, knew?'

'He's dead. Drowned, I suppose. He was washed up at Shingle Street this morning. It's all in the first edition of the *Bugle*.'

'Here, let me see!' She snatched the paper away and read the bleak, one paragraph report.

'As I said, a friend of yours. Took quite a fancy to you, didn't he?'

'Charlie was keen on the main chance.'

'Still, lucky you. I thought he looked like Michael York; you know, in *Cabaret*.'

Janet felt numb with shock. Charlie had arrived in the library about six months before, searching for a quotation to go in a piece he was writing. He had been passed on to Janet, and it had started there. He had visited the library quite a few times, for help or a chat.

After a while they had begun seeing each other regularly for meals. But Janet had not allowed the relationship to develop further, in spite of Charlie's pleas and although she had felt very flattered to have the attentions of a good-looking young man nearly ten years her junior.

Gradually she had found out more about him, for Charlie was not one to keep his personal life to himself. He had, she gathered, arrived in Suffolk to work on the local paper because he felt he had

5

been unappreciated at his job with a London weekly. In fact, he admitted, he had not left on particularly good terms.

He told her that he had been on the point of breaking a major investigative story to do with resprayed stolen cars, when the editor had called him off, and even given him a flea in his ear for working on it in the way he had done.

'Typical of today's press,' he had said bitterly, 'timid, boring and frightened of anything a bit hot to handle.'

He had been a pleasant and amusing, if rather shallow, companion. She had been at something of a loose end, and it had suited her very well. It was somewhat later, when one night she had invited him back for coffee and he had been rather drunk and disinclined to leave, that she had learned a little more.

'Go on,' he had said, 'just one night. It wouldn't hurt. You'd enjoy it, I promise you.'

She had told him he was a typically arrogant young male.

'No, honestly, I could,' he had said drunkenly, 'get you a testimonial.'

'Don't be squalid, Charlie,' she had retorted. 'I can't stand men who brag.'

He had nodded with an air of inebriated mystery, and launched into a disconnected tale which involved a woman of Janet's age, 'a tremendous looker', who had fallen heavily for Charlie in London and who, he said, had encouraged him to move to Suffolk. It was almost impossible to get a clear picture, except that the lady in question was wealthy and well-connected and would have thrown it all away for him.

'I wonder you didn't take her up on it,' she had said, only half-believing him. 'If she was that well off and crazy about you, she could have kept you for life, and you wouldn't have had to worry about unappreciative editors.'

He had then become drunkenly offended and she had finally pushed him out of the door. He had reappeared at the library the following morning with a bunch of flowers and an apology.

'What was that about?' one of her colleagues had asked.

'Oh, he got a bit drunk and boring, and when I said no, he told me what a devil he was with rich, older women.'

6

'Hm,' said her colleague, 'well I don't know about that, but I understand he does move in something of a smart set for a junior reporter on the *Bugle*. County and so on. My boyfriend, Mark that is, said he'd seen him with a party at Tatworth Hall, and you can't eat out there under about thirty quid a head, and the women were literally dripping with expensive gear.'

Janet went into the back office and read the short, uninformative news item once again. While her feelings for him may have been ambivalent, she still felt upset that anyone so young could be cut off so drastically.

She had, in fact, seen him on the previous Friday night, when they had gone into Ipswich for a curry. Charlie had been full of stifled excitement. Towards the end of the meal he had asked her:

'Do you know Shingle Street?'

'No. What part of the town is it in?'

'It's not a real street. It's the name of a place just up the coast. Do you know, something funny happened up there during the war – and after.'

'Such as what?' She had been amused by his air of mystery. As a county, Suffolk had more 'funny' areas than anywhere else in the country; nuclear bases, experimental stations, radar installations. 'There's a lot of pretty funny places here.'

'No, I mean really funny – not nice at all. Nobody knows what it was. During the war everyone in the place was evacuated, except for some kind of special outfit, and there was some sort of lab there. Then there was some kind of an accident. Rumour says people died, but there's no record of what happened anywhere. I've been trying to find out through government papers, but there's nothing among the ones published thirty years after the war. I can't find anything anywhere. But I don't think that's all. I believe something else happened there, more recently.'

'So?'

'So . . . I think I'm beginning to get on to it. I can't say much to you yet, but I've come across someone who I think knows all about it. Trouble is, he's in St Leonard's.'

At that she really did laugh out loud. He looked hurt.

'Charlie, you'll kill me. If he's in an asylum, he could believe anything. What happened? Did a spaceship land, full of little green men saying take-me-to-your-leader, or was it the place where Kronsky, the Mad Scientist, perfected his deadly death ray?'

He had been offended. 'You'll never take me seriously, will you? Not about anything. The man's called Harry, Harry Wharton, and he's absolutely rational, as sane as you or I. He's the key to it all, I'm convinced of it. Don't you see? He was put there to keep him out of the way. Now I'm off over the weekend and I'm going to take this thing further and see where I get. I could end up with a front-page story in the nationals.'

He could see her patent disbelief.

She never saw him again. As the long afternoon passed, she became more and more troubled. The newspaper item implied that he had probably gone out in a dinghy without a life-jacket and, as an inexperienced beginner, fallen in and drowned. But if Charlie was a dinghy sailor, then he had kept at least this interest of his completely secret from her.

She had, she supposed, become fond of him in a way. Poor Charlie with his delusions – the red-hot reporter leaving because he knew too much; the glamorous, sexually attractive man of the world, striving after a cushy lifestyle; the investigative journalist on the threshold of a front-page story. And yet, she thought, poor little sod, and decided to look into the matter further.

3.

She was fortunate in already having arranged to take the rest of the week off. Next day, at lunchtime, she went down to the pub where Charlie, along with most of his colleagues, usually had a snack and a pint. She recognised some people at the bar, and they immediately hailed her.

'Heard the news?' said Tony Parsons, who ran the sports pages. 'Bloody bad business.'

She nodded. 'He wasn't actually drowned, was he?'

'You're quick,' he said, taken aback. 'No, it's all a bit odd. No . . .' he continued as she tried to break in, 'he wasn't thumped on the head or knifed or anything. He's just plain dead. But not drowned. That's why our report only said he had been found dead on the beach, not drowned, although some clever clogs added a par. about the dangers of inexperienced dinghy sailors going out without life-jackets.'

'Do you think something might have happened to him because he was investigating something he shouldn't?'

'God God, woman. For the *Bugle*!' He was incredulous. 'It's only a step up from the weeklies. Our basic stuff is council meetings, local regattas, flower shows. Our occasional murders run to the chap who comes home from a heavy day on the farm to find the wife in bed with the insurance salesman. What do you think we run here – the *Sunday Times* insight team?' She began to feel foolish.

'Here,' he called to a large man sinking a pint at the bar. 'Come over here, Mick, and tell the lady how you see the *Bugle*.'

Mick smiled. 'We're apolitical. That is, we're for the government when it's Tory, and our editorial policy is to support law and order and all that, in case mobs of screaming rioters from Grundsburgh or Little Easton take to the lanes of Suffolk. We tolerate our Labour MP because deep down inside we know he's one of us; and anyway, if we were too rude, we'd lose advertising. As for crime, well, there's a little shoplifting, a bit of breaking and entering, a spot of poaching. The two biggest stories we had last year when a churchwarden out at Twitchett made an improper suggestion to a choir boy and when a girl at Tesbury's was found putting her hand in the till.'

'Charlie's obviously been selling you some of his yarns,' Tony broke in. 'You know, the Ace Reporter who Tried to Tell All and Had to Leave.'

'Did you see much of him outside office hours?'

'Well, of course he'd only been here about six months. He was a funny chap. A bit of a lad for the women – no offence meant,' he added hastily. 'But he rather gave the impression that he had it made most of the time. Oh God, I'm making it even worse.'

'Not with me, he didn't,' Janet said firmly.

'Actually,' continued Tony, 'he moved in circles above our station. Don't know how he did it on a *Bugle* salary, but we knew he ate out in pretty classy places and got himself invited around the place by the local nobs.'

'It must have been for the sake of his pretty face,' suggested Mick.

She felt it was time to move on. But before going, she asked what they thought would happen at the inquest. Mick had spoken to the police. 'Very little at this stage. There'll be evidence of identification; the chap who found him will probably say his bit; the police will say theirs and ask for an adjournment pending further inquiries. And that will be that, I imagine. Presumably they'll know in a day or two why he died. Perhaps he had a dicky heart or something even he didn't know about.'

Meanwhile, John Latimer was also pursuing his inquiries. He had gone back to the editor of the *Bugle* and found out from him the name of Spencer's previous paper, a South London weekly, and had then contacted its editor.

The editor of the *Wandsworth Weekly* had been tart at the mention of Charlie Spencer's name, although he had altered his tone somewhat when he heard the news. Yes, Spencer had worked on the *Weekly* for nearly two years. He had arrived on it straight from one of the redbrick universities. He had seemed to be quite promising – at first.

'Only at first?' Latimer asked.

'Well,' said the editor, 'he really was a big-headed lad. He got on to a story about stolen cars being resprayed and reprocessed in London, and it all blew up in our faces.'

'Sounds pretty useful to me,' Latimer replied, 'I'd imagine the boys from the Met would have been only too pleased if he'd dug out something like that.'

The boys from the Met, it emerged, had been far from pleased. Charlie had been told quite firmly that the police had the matter in hand and that he was to leave it alone. But in spite of that and against the editor's strict orders, he had carried blithely on. Worse, he had been less than clever in the way he had gone about his investigations, and it had ended pretty disastrously. Charlie had received some sharp and convincing threats to lay off, and the thieves had been fully alerted. The police had had to act much sooner than they planned, and the net result was that all the big boys had got away, leaving only the little ones to be taken.

'We didn't actually sack him,' said the *Weekly* editor, 'but we made it pretty clear that he wasn't very popular. I was relieved when he left of his own accord. Between his crass notions of investigative reporting and a West End lifestyle that left him permanently late for work, even he must have known the writing was on the wall.'

'Does the *Weekly* pay enough for a West End lifestyle, then?' Latimer inquired in some surprise.

'Does it Hell,' responded the editor with feeling. 'It wouldn't even keep me in that kind of company. But Charlie spent half his time moving around with a set of people and frittering the night away in hotspots that needed an awful lot more than a *Weekly* salary to support.'

Latimer had thanked him and thoughtfully replaced the receiver. Then he picked it up again and got through to a friend in the Met.

'Can you find me anything you might have on file about a car racket in Wandsworth. It came to a head about six months ago.'

'That's a tall order. South London's one big car racket.'

'No, but this one went wrong. Some young, bright lad on the *Wandsworth Weekly* blew the story before your lot were ready and ended up threatened with a variety of painful treatments to boot. Can you see if anybody involved would be prepared to actually carry out the threats? The lad's turned up dead on a Suffolk beach.'

'It's murder then.'

'No, actually we don't think so. No signs at all of foul play. He wasn't even drowned. But it's as well to check. Ring me back when you know a bit more, there's a good chap.'

Some weeks before, Janet had had a dental appointment, and Charlie had offered her the key of his flat 'in case you feel a bit rough after having your tooth out'. He pressed it on her, saying he was pretty careless with keys and was always getting them cut.

She thought the police were bound to search his flat, but she

11

decided to take a chance. Her anonymous-looking old car would hardly stand out in the service road beside the flats in whch he had lived. Nor, she felt ruefully, would she draw even a passing glance with her untidy hair and porridge-coloured raincoat.

All the same, she felt a little uneasy when she unlocked the door. It was very quiet and it did not look as if the police had disturbed it, even if they had been there. It had the air of a bachelor flat, stark and furnished with only the scrappiest of necessities. Heaps of old newspapers lay all over the small sitting-room, some with stories marked for cutting. There was nothing significant there; the stories covered a wide range of topics.

In the tiny kitchen, the dirty plates and mugs were still piled in the sink. Everything was left as if the owner were about to return at any moment. The bedroom was strewn with clothes, clean, partly worn and dirty, all thrown in untidy heaps on chairs. Not surprisingly, the wardrobe was almost empty.

There were lots of books. She went quickly through a cardboard box containing new editions. Examining the weird selection, from *Teach Yourself Psycho-Analysis* and *Everything You Ever Wanted to Know About Woodwork* to *Clorinda: Woman of Shame*, she assumed that these had been handed out by the books editor for one-line reviews. The reviewer could then get half their value by getting them to the trade bookshops in time.

A set of bookshelves held a small library of reference books and modern novels, and many more science fiction paperbacks and spy thrillers. There were also books from Charlie's youth: the Arthur Ransome stories and a complete set of James Bond in paperback. She drew out *Doctor No* and smiled to see on the flyleaf: 'Charles Freemond Spencer, 27 Crayburn Gardens, London SW4, England, The World, The Universe'. She put it back, but it did not slide in easily. Peering behind to look, she discovered a large, hardback book behind the paperbacks.

It was hardly an obvious choice. It was called *Delayed Toxic Effects of Chemical Warfare Agents* by Taylor and Franks, published in London in 1975. Inside the front cover was a piece of envelope across which was written 'Harry' in pencil. The name rang a distant bell and then she remembered that the mystery man in St

Leonard's had been called Harry. On impulse, she put the book in her bag.

The flat yielded little else. She found the telephone and telephone directory and noted the number of St Leonard's in her own address book, noticing with some disbelief the colossal breasts of the lady on the calendar immediately above the phone. She was lying on a fur rug, wearing only a pair of patent leather boots, and her ample anatomy was covered in telephone numbers.

The naked lady prompted another thought. Feeling rather furtive, Janet approached Charlie's desk and gingerly pulled open the top drawer. Like everything else in Charlie's flat, it was untidy. But on the top lay a pile of letters in a rubber band. The paper was expensive, possibly handmade, and she was about to pick them up when doubts overcame her. It really wasn't any concern of hers. She decided she had better go.

She was thankful that she did. As she came down the second flight of stairs, she almost collided with a tall fiftyish man on his way up, slightly ahead of two uniformed policemen. Both parties apologised, and Latimer carried on up the stairs without even a backward glance. Janet went thankfully to her car, noting the police car parked further down the service road. She drove hurriedly away.

The police search of the flat was much more methodical.

'God,' said Constable Jones in disgust, 'what a hole. Fancy a young man like that getting a nice new flat like this and then living like a pig.'

'It's bachelor days, sir,' said the sergeant with a grin.

'Hm,' replied Latimer, whose own wife kept his house immaculate, 'you'd have thought his mother would have taught him basic household habits. It hardly fits with what we've been told about his high-flying social image.'

'Possibly his attractions lay elsewhere,' suggested the sergeant.

They carried on through the sitting-room, bedroom, kitchen, finding nothing of significance. Charlie's desk was in the rather wide hall which he had used as a kind of office.

'Drawers aren't locked,' the constable said to the sergeant and Latimer.

'Well, take a look.' Latimer began looking through Charlie's books.

The drawers were full of heaps of bills, paid and unpaid, typing paper, envelopes, a few empty files, yellowed newspaper clippings, handouts, press releases – and the neatly bundled letters. The sergeant took off the rubber band and began to read. Some time passed as Latimer became absorbed, despite himself, in one of Charlie's paperbacks.

He was brought back to earth by his sergeant.

'Good grief, sir, you'd better take a look at these. Talk about hot stuff . . .'

Latimer took the first couple of letters and glanced at them. The thick, cream, laid paper had no address. Each letter was headed only 'Chelsea' on each page. Nor was there any date, simply 'Monday' or 'Thursday', or some other day of the week. It was clear that, whoever the writer was, she and Charlie had been having a passionate affair. The lady's style ran to the kind in those paperbacks Latimer had once heard described as 'bodice rippers'. The heavily etched paragraphs dwelt in detail on nights of love and how Charlie made her feel like a young girl again. Systematically the chief inspector and sergeant went through the letters.

It was obvious fairly quickly that the woman, who signed herself 'F', did not live in London all the time. She appeared to have a home in the country, visiting London regularly for a few days at a time, where she had her own Chelsea flat. It was equally obvious from the letters that there was a husband in the background who knew nothing of his wife's activities and must never know.

The letters supported the suggestions from the editor of the *Wandsworth Weekly* that Charlie had led a vigorous and expensive night-life. The couple had gone to parties, out to restaurants, danced at smart night spots, apparently secure in the knowledge that the lady's husband would be unaware of what was going on. Some of the letters had accompanied gifts – and gifts of no mean order, from expensive clothing to a gold cigarette case. 'F' was paying for it all because, as she put it, 'you give me so very, very much'.

'Bloody ponce,' muttered the sergeant, darkly.

Towards the end of the pile the tone of the letters suddenly changed. For the first time there was a note of panic, and it seemed to follow some communication that Charlie was moving to Suffolk. This, it seemed, would not suit the lady one bit; she begged him not to 'spoil it all'.

'Moving on to the home patch,' remarked Latimer. 'She must actually live around here somewhere. I wonder who the hell she is?'

The last two letters were abrupt and far from passionate. The very last gave a clue, for it was actually signed 'Yours, Frances', and more significantly it was headed 'Great Horton'.

'Any thoughts?' asked Latimer.

'Frances . . . Frances . . . Horton. Good God, sir, it couldn't be old Stimpson's wife? The JP? Er – they do say,' he said somewhat embarrassed, 'she's a bit of a goer. In fact when she was young, they called her the Stembridge bicycle.'

'The Stembridge what?'

'Bicycle, sir. It's a . . . well, a kind of popular term for a bit of stuff that puts herself about. She was Frances Chatworth before she married Stimpson, and old Chatworth owned half the land round Stembridge, so she was a wealthy woman in her own right when she married Terence Stimpson.'

'It's beginning to come back to me too. Bring the letters back to the office then,' said Latimer. 'I suppose it means we might well have to tackle old Stimpson, and I can't say I find that idea very appealing. He's a crusty old devil at the best of times. Let's hope it won't be necessary and that by now the forensic lads will be able to tell us Spencer died from natural causes.'

4.

At Stembridge police station, Latimer and Sergeant Chapman found the police doctor already waiting for them.

'Well,' said the doctor, 'I've had the report back from London but it doesn't take us much further on.'

'What did they find?'

'Nothing – nothing at all. There was no sign of any kind of violence, no poisoning. They did all the usual tests for just about everything. Do you know any more?'

'A few things. It seems he left his last paper under a bit of a cloud – poked his nose into business the Met lads were already working on and loused it up.'

'They must have been pleased.'

'Not as pleased as the villains concerned. He seems to have been threatened with something nasty as a result. Also, it appears he was more than a bit of a ladies' man. He was running some expensive female on the side up in London, and it looks as if he may have followed her down here.'

'So far as the medical aspect is concerned,' continued the doctor, 'the *Bugle* is part of one of the big newspaper groups. When any of the papers takes on somebody new, then he or she has to have a full medical by the company doctor in London before they start. Because of the pension and all that jazz.'

'Six months ago Spencer was seen in Harley Street by a Dr Lomas, who gave him a very thorough check-up. He was a perfectly healthy young man. Heart, lungs, blood pressure, all quite, quite normal. Dr Lomas has his X-rays, the notes of his check-up. There is absolutely no chance of unsuspected heart trouble being undiagnosed. His kidneys were OK, lungs clear – he didn't smoke – he couldn't have been fitter.'

'You did say something about scratches or abrasions.'

'They might have made him jump at the time but they certainly

16

couldn't cause anything serious. He'd hardly have developed something like tetanus within such a short time and anyway there'd have been something to show for it. No, it really is a mystery. The only oddity I noticed was a slight muscle contraction before death, but it still doesn't add up to anything.'

Latimer drew his notes together. 'Presumably you will say at the inquest that there was no apparent cause of death and that you have no reason to suspect foul play was involved? I imagine the coroner will want an adjournment, though, pending further inquiries. Then if nothing comes up, I imagine it will eventually be death by cause or causes unknown.'

'Are you still looking into it?'

'For the time being. I'm waiting for a call from London and we've had a go at his flat. Nothing there, pretty squalid state he lived in, but I suppose that's young people these days. But we did find some fairly torrid correspondence.'

'Perhaps a jealous husband bumped him off.'

'If he did, then he used one of those strange poisons known only to writers of detective novels – the sort that fade away and leave no trace.'

After the doctor had gone, he looked through the slim file on Spencer and added the medical reports from the police doctor and from Dr Lomas. There was a brief statement from Eddie Hutchinson on his finding the body, a note from Spencer's Ipswich editor on what was known of his background and his working habits, and a statement from Spencer's father who had been down to the mortuary that morning to identify his son's body and then returned immediately to London. He had not seen his son, he said, since he moved away from London and had seen little of him before that, as he had only occasionally turned up at the family home. He seemed completely at a loss, and shocked. No, he could think of no reason at all for suicide, even if there was anything to suggest that his son had taken such action. He had been a perfectly normal lad.

'In fact,' thought Latimer to himself, 'the only really unusual thing he seems to have done in his whole life is to be found dead on Shingle Street beach.' At this point his telephone rang and he was put through again to his friend from New Scotland Yard.

'Well,' he told Latimer, 'we've checked it out as far as we could and I think we've hit on what you meant. It seems there was a pretty lucrative stolen car business being run from a garage in Wandsworth. Garage was apparently impeccable, classy goods on the forecourt, filling station, all that sort of thing, workshops which were perfectly genuine – but behind them were more, where pretty expensive stolen cars came in for a respray.

'Our lads had just about got it taped and were ready to go when your intrepid hero rushed in with both flat feet. And by the time our mob got there, all we found was a couple of very minor villains and no vehicles except genuine repair jobs. It seems your lad reported afterwards that he'd had a few threatening phone calls, and some character had bounced him against a pub wall a couple of week later and told him a few home truths. But we know who that was, and anyway he's been having full board at the expense of Her Majesty at Winson Green in Birmingham for the last two months on another charge. Rural Suffolk would hardly be his cup of tea – he'd feel isolated on Wandsworth Common.'

Latimer thanked him and turned his attention elsewhere. He was a man who found the phrase 'community policing' annoyingly trendy; he had always seen the police as part of the local community. He himself was a local man who had risen through the ranks. He lived just outside Stembridge and his children went to local schools. Young policemen looking for a macho work style of screaming police cars and blue flashing lights found themselves walking the beat and attending courses on everything from juvenile delinquency to social work.

Janet drove back to Stembridge, her mind only half on the road. It was high summer, and on either side of the narrow lanes, huge drifts of poppies stretched into the distance in a flood. Preoccupied as she was, she stopped the car to look at a lake of them washing around a small cottage. Beyond, a haze hung over the river, and the masts of small boats were perfectly still. It was no place, she felt, for death.

Parking her car behind her house, she saw the landlord of the Blue Lion walking his dog. He was known for his ability to pick up local gossip faster than anybody else in the neighbourhood and was called, behind his back, the Stembridge Clarion.

It was clear that he could not wait to speak to her. 'Heard about your young friend,' he shouted as she locked the car door. 'Quite a tragedy. You'll miss him, won't you? Pretty odd place to go, wasn't it. There's nothing there but a few old houses, marshes, a bit of beach.'

'You've lived here all your life, haven't you? Did you ever hear any stories about Shingle Street – you know, funny things that happened during the war?'

'Why, I suppose most people have heard something, though damned if I know what. They do say as something nasty happened up there during the war. It was all closed off, you see. They took the people away and rehoused them inland, and a lot of government folk went and lived there. They built some kind of a hall for themselves. It's still there but it doesn't get used for anything now that I know of.'

'Then after the war I suppose everybody came back?'

'Not for some time after and then there were so many odd tales that some families never did go back. They'd wired off all that marshland by the road down to the place, and the huts and stuff they had there were still used much later on – oh, perhaps fifteen years ago, perhaps less than that. And there were bloody great notices saying, Keep Out – Ministry of Defence. But we're used to that sort of thing around here and nobody took any notice of it.'

'Is there anything there now?'

'Nothing much. People are back living in a few of the houses. Some are let to summer visitors – though they must be mad to my way of thinking. The water's always stone cold and the wind bites to the bone. Most of the huts on the marshes have gone, I think, but then I've not been up that way much recently. Most of those who do go are there for the sea fishing, and they're welcome to sit out there with a lantern at night and freeze to death trying to catch a cod . . .'

She watched him continue down the street and then, on impulse, decided to go to police headquarters. She knew that a Chief

19

Inspector Latimer was in charge of the case. She had been told as much by the *Bugle* reporters.

She asked the desk sergeant if she could see him for a few minutes, saying that she was a friend of Charles Spencer. Within a few minutes he had returned and asked if she would like to come in and see the inspector. She recognised him immediately as the man she had seen on the stairs outside Charlie's flat, but if he recognised her, he gave no sign of it.

'It's thoughtful of you to come along, Mrs Simms,' he said, offering her a seat. 'Was he a close friend?' For a moment he wondered if she was the writer of the letters, but then discarded the thought. She would hardly change her name, nor did she look the type, but then he was beginning to wonder just how many older women Spencer had been running. The woman was obviously concerned.

'I didn't know him all that well,' she began cautiously. 'I work in the library and we met when he wanted something looked up. Afterwards we had a few meals out together – I'm divorced by the way. But I was very shocked when I heard the news.'

'Did he talk to you much about his life?'

She smiled ruefully. 'To be honest, I thought most of it was fantasising. He told me he'd been on the brink of pulling off some terrific scoop in London and then the editor got cold feet and wouldn't let him go ahead. Oh, and once when he got a little drunk and – not to put too fine a point on it – a little difficult, he did tell me he'd had some kind of affair with some rich and beautiful older woman who had promised him anything he wanted. I couldn't take it too seriously, though.'

Latimer regarded her thoughtfully. 'There does seem to be something in it. There often is with these people who like to see themselves in leading roles. He did get involved with a story in London, but from what I understand he made a total botch of it by rushing in without any thought and without taking his editor's advice.'

'That makes sense.'

'It also seems he might have been having something of a fling. I suppose he didn't tell you her name?'

'No. Had he been going to, I'd have put him off. I told him I didn't find men who bragged particularly attractive. There is one other thing. He seemed really genuinely excited when I saw him on Friday night.'

'You saw him as recently as that?'

'Yes, we had a curry in Ipswich. He was full of some story he was going to work on which he was convinced would make his name and be front-page stuff in the nationals. He was very mysterious about it though.'

'Did he tell you what it was about?'

She hesitated, and then some sense made her draw back from complete honesty. 'Not really. But he did say something about Shingle Street, and that was where he was found, wasn't it? That's what made me come to you.'

'It was very thoughtful of you. We don't honestly see any point in carrying on inquiries for much longer. While we can't find out how he died, it does seem to have been natural death, however sudden. We may try to chase up this woman friend, if we can find her, and see if she can tell us anything. But then that will probably be as far as we can go.'

'And Shingle Street?'

'I can't honestly see that has any significance. But, if you do think of anything else, don't hesitate to get in touch.'

She smiled and left.

After she had gone, Latimer pulled out the heap of letters once more. He could see that the woman had been far from happy at the prospect of her young lover moving in on the doorstep. His sergeant's suggestion that it might be Frances Stimpson did make some sense, and he called for him.

'I don't know too much about either of them. Can you fill me in a bit?'

'Well, as I told you, she was fairly hot stuff and old man Chatworth must have been fast running out of possible husband material. She was all right for a good time and not particularly fussy with it, and then down comes Stimpson – having made his pile in merchant banking – looking for a manor house and someone to go with it. And there you are. He didn't know anything about her,

21

which is just as well. He's a devil on the bench, as you know – no time at all for human weakness. She was getting fed up and looking for security and a rich older man, and Bob's your uncle. There's never been any talk here. She must have kept her little excursions for London. But I wonder just how her old man would take the idea of her not only having a lover but carrying on with him here, on his own doorstep. He may be a JP, but he's not a very nice character.'

'Maybe not, but I'm still not very happy about this one and I think we'd better look in on the amorous Mrs Frances Stimpson tomorrow. Oh, by the way, I had one of the librarians in just now, asking about Spencer. You may know her – she's called Janet Simms, thirty-five-ish, dark, rather bright. It seems she too was a friend of his.'

'Good grief, it makes you wonder if he had any time at all to do his job. Did he have a retinue of mature ladies?'

'She was quite firm about there being none of that. But it appears he told her something of his troubles in London and also bragged on one occasion about his having a fling with some well-known local woman.'

'And she came to suggest it might have something to do with his death?'

'In part, but she also told me he said he was working on some amazing scoop and she asked if I knew anything about Shingle Street. Not just the fact that his body was found there, but that this story, whatever it is, was connected with the place in some way.'

The sergeant pondered. 'I can't say it means anything to me. Wasn't there some kind of research place there during the war? Oh yes, of course, there was supposed to have been some kind of funny business that went on there then, but it must be all of forty years ago. Hardly the stuff of front-page stories.'

'Hardly. Well, there's more to do than sit here speculating about Spencer. I'll have a look at that Forsythe file again, the case comes to court next week.'

The Forsythe case involved a petty swindler and a spate of forged cheques drawn with a stolen bank card. Latimer was about half-way through when a constable knocked at the door.

'There's a reporter outside, sir. He would like to see you.'

'What about? It can't be the *Bugle*, the editor knows nearly as much as we do about the Spencer case.'

'This chap says that it is about Spencer and that's why he wants a word. But it's not the *Bugle*. He's from the *Daily Clarion*.'

With ill grace, Latimer asked for him to be shown in and with less than his usual courtesy asked him to take a seat.

The reporter was about forty, tall with with the incipient belly of those who drink deep and eat badly. He was greying at the temples and his eyes were tired and puffy. He looked as if he could do with some sleep.

'My name's Bill Baxter, Chief Inspector, from the *Clarion*. Thank you for seeing me. I just wanted to find out what you could tell me about the death of this lad, Spencer.'

'I don't want to sound unhelpful but there's really very little to tell. He was found dead a few miles north of here, on a beach at a place called Shingle Street. He had not been drowned although he had been in the water for a little while. There are no signs of foul play. Forensic tests have shown nothing and there is no obvious cause of death. He seems to have been a pretty ordinary sort of lad, if a bit of a bragger. It seems he ran into some trouble with his editor when he worked in South London.'

'Most of us do that from time to time. It's an occupational hazard.'

'Might I ask why the *Clarion* is interested?'

'Certainly. You see Charlie used to string for us a bit . . .'

Latimer looked blank.

'What I mean is, he used to tip us off over stories he thought might interest us. It's not strictly correct under the terms of his contract but all the local-paper boys do it. It gives them a bit of money on the side and sometimes gives them a bit of an in later on if they try for a job in Fleet Street.

'On Saturday morning he rang me at the office and said he might have something of real interest for me on Monday morning. I asked him what it was and he wouldn't say, just that he was following up something that would make a very good story. He sounded quite excited. Now I don't say all the stuff he'd tipped us off about has been earth-shattering, page-one material, but most of it was sound enough.'

'You surprise me. His reputation before he came here was the reverse.'

'He must have improved then. So I was waiting to hear from him yesterday and then I picked up a note from PA – the Press Association – that he'd been found dead. I told my news editor and he said to get down here and look into it. So here I am.'

'I see. But I think you'll find you're wasting your time. Check with the *Bugle*, but I can't think he would have been working on a story so dangerous he could have ended up dead. The idea's ridiculous. We're checking out one or two features of the case, trying to find out who he knew and so on, but we're not expecting it to go much further. If I were you, I'd go back to London. And if there are any more developments – which I very much doubt – I'll let you know.'

Baxter looked unconvinced. 'Thanks for the information. I believe you. I'm sure you're right. But I still think I'll stick around for a day or two. You never know, something may turn up.'

5.

Janet had intended to spend the time while her children were away catching up on her own reading, working in the garden and going for walks, blissfully set free from the discipline of regular meals and cooking, washing and shopping for a family. She resented her own feelings about Spencer. It was nothing to do with her. The police were virtually certain there was nothing sinister about his death. Yet the sense that something was very wrong would not leave her.

She dipped into the book she had taken from his flat and realised that it was a standard work on the subject. It explained, in highly technical language, the principles on which chemical weapons were based, but many of the terms used were unfamiliar to her and the dictionary proved useless.

The pencilled slip of paper with the name Harry on it reminded her of Charlie's story of the mystery man in St Leonard's, and she decided it could do no harm if she followed it up.

It took a little while, when she telephoned the hospital, to find out exactly where he was, since she did not know the name of his ward. But the sister in charge finally told her that yes, Mr Wharton was very well, he was not in a closed ward and he could receive visitors. She was a relative? Yes, Janet lied, a niece.

When she arrived that afternoon bringing fruit and, she trusted, a convincing manner, she was appalled at the sight of the building. It was large and forbidding, a cluster of brick extensions and portakabins surrounding what looked like an old Victorian work-house. The inside smelt of disinfectant and other, less pleasant smells. It was dark and dingy.

The nurse who led her through the maze of corridors caught her mood.

'They told us it was an impossible place ten years ago. We've been going to have a new hospital ever since but nothing's been done. If anything, it's got worse.'

'However do you manage?'

'With difficulty . . . There's not enough nurses, not enough facilities, not enough anything. Mr Wharton's one of the lucky ones. His group of wards has a new dayroom donated by the League of Friends.'

She handed Janet over to a sister who led her into the dayroom. It was a bleak rectangle, built with visible economy. A large window filled most of the far wall. Ranged opposite to it was a row of identical vinyl armchairs, neatly spaced about a foot apart, and each occupied by someone old. Some muttered quietly to them-selves, most just stared blankly ahead. A large colour television set rippled meaninglessly away in front of the window, showing part of an Open University course.

Harry Wharton sat at the far end. As soon as she saw him, she realised the difference. He looked like a shrivelled gnome and his limbs never stopped twitching, but his eyes were clear and intelligent.

25

'Another visitor for you, Mr Wharton,' said the sister in a loud, slow voice. 'Aren't you lucky? That's the second one in a week after such a long time without. Now mind you behave yourself – none of your silly nonsense.'

She rustled away, her shoes creaking on the polished floor.

Janet pulled up an ordinary chair and carefully set her bag of fruit down beside Harry.

'I expect you're wondering who I am. I'm a friend of Charlie, the fair young man who came to see you last week.'

His eyes regarded her shrewdly.

'He's dead, isn't he? Yes, they do let some of us see the papers in here, even if they think we're too bloody daft to understand them.'

'That's what I've come about. I work in the library at Stembridge and Charlie used to come in from time to time. We became quite friendly. The night before he died he mentioned you. He told me he was following up a story and that you had helped him with it, and that it had something to do with Shingle Street. He was found dead there, you know, on the beach. The tide had washed him in.'

Harry nodded.

'Nobody seems to know how or why he died. He must have been at Shingle Street on the Saturday night and I'm worried about it, Mr Wharton. Did you tell him anything that could explain any of it? I've no right at all to ask you, I realise that. But it worries me.'

'Why do you really want to know?' asked Harry. 'And why should I tell you?'

'Because it doesn't feel right, Mr Wharton – Harry. I don't like things that don't feel right. Charlie was a terrible romancer, but I've been wondering if this time he was telling the truth. He said that he had come across a story he might be able to sell to the national papers; and if he had, then I want to know even more why he died, because it seems a remarkable coincidence – too neat to be true. Did he ask you about what happened there during the war?'

'He did, but I couldn't tell him. I reckon there's only a few people who could and they're not talking. No, what I told him about was the accident afterwards.'

'What accident?'

'The one that bloody well put me in here.'

'It's an impressive place,' Latimer said to Sergeant Chapman, as the car pulled up outside the imposing, thatched, pink house where the Stimpsons lived. They had made sure that Terence Stimpson was safely out of the way, presiding over the local bench.

They rang the bell.

A neatly-dressed, grey-haired woman, obviously a housekeeper, answered it.

'I'm sorry to trouble you,' said Latimer. 'I'm Chief Inspector John Latimer from Stembridge police headquarters and this is Sergeant Chapman. We were wondering if Mrs Frances Stimpson was in, and if we might have a word with her.'

The woman regarded them doubtfully.

'What is it about?'

'Just routine inquiries, madam.'

She disappeared for some time, and then they heard the brisk clatter of heels along a parquet floor and Frances Stimpson emerged. She was carrying a shallow basket, half-filled with flowers, and she was, as the sergeant had suggested, 'still something of a looker'. She had the leanness of someone who took expensive care of herself. Her hair was tinted and well cut, her make-up perfect. She wore a green trouser suit which Latimer recognised must have cost old Stimpson a packet. A rope of pearls was knotted around her silk scarf.

'I'm sorry to trouble you, madam,' he sid politely, 'but we're making some inquiries into the death of a Mr Charles Spencer. You may have heard that his body was found on the beach at Shingle Street on Monday morning.'

'I did read something about a body but I didn't really take it in,' she replied coolly. 'I can't imagine why you want to ask me about him. I've never even heard of him.'

'You're quite sure about that?'

'Absolutely sure.'

'I'm sorry, Mrs Stimpson, but we have reason to believe that the young man was a friend of yours.'

'What did you say his name was? Spencer – I suppose it's just about possible we might have met somewhere or other, at a party or visiting friends. But the name still doesn't ring a bell. What did he do?'

'He was a journalist on the local paper.'

'I can't imagine that some local cub reporter would be likely to move in the same circles I do.'

Latimer had to admire her. There was not a crack in the composure. As a performance it was faultless.

'But you knew him before, didn't you? In London?'

'Really, Chief Inspector, this conversation isn't getting us anywhere. I've already told you I didn't know the young man, and now if you'll excuse me . . .'

Latimer took the bundle of letters out of his pocket.

'Perhaps you'd just like to glance at these before you go.'

This time the reaction was immediate. The colour drained from her face. 'You'd better come through here,' she said abruptly.

She led them into her husband's study and sat down beside a handsome oak desk. Latimer began laying the letters down carefully, one at a time, in front of her.

'You did write these, didn't you?'

'Oh God. Yes, I did. I never intended it to go so far. I got very bored here and I have my own flat in London. My husband doesn't like it but he knows I have to go away regularly or I just get bored to death. I met Charlie at Tramp, the night club. He was with a party of people I knew slightly – he was a bit of a social climber, you know. We danced a bit, had a few drinks, and it went on from there. Just a bit of fun, you know, nothing serious. He was a very, very pretty young man, officer.'

'Did your husband suspect anything then?'

'Good God, no. He's a very difficult man, very hard and very puritanical.' She looked at their faces.

Latimer said, 'I gather you weren't at all happy when you knew Spencer was going to work locally.'

'I begged him not to. I told him that if he did, it would have to finish. There was no question of my seeing him here. Whatever small excitements I have sought, I've always kept them strictly to London.'

'But he didn't take your advice?'

'No, he didn't. He managed to get himself invited to all kinds of places where normally someone of that sort wouldn't go. As I said, he was very attractive and he could insinuate himself into most people's graces. The more offhand I was, the more he tried to pursue it, and eventually I think my husband did begin to be suspicious.'

'Did your husband say anything to you?'

'He asked me what I thought the young man was after, and for the first time I don't think he believed me when I said I didn't know. I assured him that I wasn't encouraging him.'

'And he believed you?'

'At first. But later I'm not so sure. He's behaved very oddly for the last three or four weeks. He's hardly spoken to me and when he has, it's been very cold.'

'Is your husband a violent man?'

'He's eminently respectable. You must know he's a JP, a pillar of the community.'

'That's not what I asked you. I asked if he was violent?'

She smiled bitterly and pulled aside the wide silk scarf and its rope of pearls. Clearly visible on the side of her neck were dark marks, gradually fading.

'Look for yourself. That's a small memento of our last little tiff.'

After making sure where they could contact her again, Latimer and Chapman left.

'Who'd have thought it?' Chapman said to Latimer.

'You can't tell. Wife-bashing isn't confined to the working classes as we are led to suppose. All kinds of people do it – bankers, teachers, even judges.'

'Fancy a woman like that putting up with it. But perhaps she likes it?'

'Possibly it gives her a thrill but I doubt it. Anyway, all it's proved is that she and Spencer were lovers and that her husband may or may not have known about it and that he is prone to violence, but we're still back with the fact that there were no marks of violence on the body.'

6.

At St Leonard's Hospital the tea was being brought around on a trolley. The woman pushing the trolley had been slightly friendlier than the ward sister and had offered Janet a cup while she was serving Harry.

Once she had gone out of earshot, Harry bent forward:

'I'll tell you what happened to me, same as I told the young fellow. But if I do, don't you go and die on me.'

Suppressing a slight shudder, Janet said she would try not to.

'Now,' said Harry, 'the young chap asked me first what happened at Shingle Street during the war. I couldn't tell him nothing about that. All I know is what everyone knows. All the people there were moved out and sometime something happened down there but nobody knows what. A few have asked but they didn't get nowhere.'

'I came into it later, around fifteen or sixteen years ago. There was still some kind of government work going on then in huts on the right-hand side of the road as you come across into Shingle Street. There was also underground places too, like they've got at the air bases or had in my day anyway.

'Well, I was working as a plumber at the time for a local firm that did all kinds of pipework and so on, and one day the boss said there was a job going up at Shingle Street. We did a fair bit of work for the military, one way and another, so I never thought anything of it.

'A team of four of us went up there: me, Tommy Giggs from Stembridge, Pete Burrows – he was a smashing amateur footballer that chap, could've played for Ipswich – and old Johnny Fenn who could plumb anything into anything. It were quite a big job. There was a kind of laboratory place in one of the huts and they wanted us to put in some new drains and half a dozen new sinks and plumb them in. Then there were some repair work to be done on two or three other things and one sink in particular had a faulty trap which needed replacing.

'Well, we spent a couple of days on all the new work and then, on the last day, we started on the old sinks and Johnny Fenn tackled the trap on an old sink. It were real stiff and in the end both Pete and I had to have a go before we could get it off. Anyway we got it off and put the new one on and finished the work and went home. Pete and old Johnny Fenn were both saying they'd got bad heads in the van on the way home, but we all laughed and said it were the beer in the Blue Lion – straight out of the Deben and into the pumps on the bar they say round here, rubbish stuff compared to our local brew.

'When I got up the following morning I really did feel rough, but as it was Friday I said to the wife I'd go in to work and take it easy over the weekend. I'd just gone out to the car when something really hit me. I managed to crawl in to the wife and she got the doctor and he said it were a stroke and sent me to hospital. I come out of that a bit, though, and the top chap up there said he didn't reckon it were a stroke, and when I were a bit better he sent me to London.

'By this time I were shaking like I am now. Then another top chap saw me and he said he were very sorry but it were a brain tumour and he reckoned there were little he could do. So back I went to hospital here.

'I were still getting terrible pains in my chest, so yet another fellow was sent for and he said they'd decided there was nothing wrong with my brain. In fact I were a bit of a mystery. There was nothing wrong they could find with my heart either and after a bit they sent me home and told me to take it easy.

'But I didn't get much better after that. I'd come over queer and weak and faint and my legs go weak when I stand for long. But after a bit I asked my wife why Pete and Johnny and Tommy had never been to see me or ask how I was, and at first she didn't want to say anything. Then she told me they was dead, all dead.'

'*All* of them?'

'Aye. Old Johnny Fenn, he died on the day I were took bad and they put heart failure on his death certificate, which I suppose is right. We all die of that in the end,' he commented drily. 'Now Tommy and Pete, they was rushed up to hospital in London and their wives never did get no clear tale of what happened. They said Tommy died of a stroke and that Pete had a heart attack, he must have had a weak heart. Weak heart! Those as said that must have been weak in the head, he were a great, strapping chap. Football were his life.

'So I thought to myself, something bloody funny's happened here and it hit me straight away it must have been something to do with that laboratory place, some kind of a germ or something which made us all bad. Yet I'd not seen nothing nor smelled anything. The old sinks and pipes looked quite clean and dry. Anyway I thinks about it a bit more, and then I gets the missis to write to the Ministry of Defence what owned the place, saying I'd been took bad there after working in the place and did they know what it might be? I also said that if I had caught something working there then perhaps I was due for some compensation?'

'And?'

'Well, the next thing was a real posh man from the Ministry and some clever Ministry doctor called. They told us they'd looked into my case and there was no real cause for any of it and there wasn't nothing up at Shingle Street that were harmful. The doctor he examined me and wrote some things down but he never said nothing at all and after a bit they went away.

'I'm a stubborn sort of a chap and I thought that's just not good enough, so I wrote again. I wrote to my MP and all, though he's about as much good as a piece of frozen cod, and when we still heard nothing my missis wrote again to the chap what had been down to see us and said she was going to see a solicitor.

'The next day they was back again and this time they was real nasty. They told me there was nothing really badly wrong with me. It was me nerves, they said. I was depressed and having fancies and the dizziness and sweats and shakes and so on was all in my mind. Probably I'd had some kind of mild heart attack. The doctor chap then said why didn't I go into the local mental hospital and see if they could help me, and I said I were as sane as he was, and he upped and went.

'When the missis came back from seeing them out she were raging. She said the doctor chap had said why didn't she agree to have me put away in the mental hospital for a bit so they could sort me out. All she would have to do would be to sign the paper they'd brought with them and that would be that. She showed them the door.'

'We never got no further after that. But the more I've thought about it since, the more I've thought there was some kind of an accident up there that day what was hushed up.'

It sounded all too probable, Janet thought. 'So how did you end up here, Harry?'

'The missis went and died – cancer. Me son lives in London and he and his daughter live their own life, they don't bother much with us. But he wrote again to the Ministry and they just said I were barmy and if he was really bothered about me, he'd sign the papers and they'd try and get me right in here. That were five years ago, and I've been in here ever since. Look, gal, if you can find out anything let me know. Perhaps I'd get enough money to get out of this place . . .'

'Time to go now,' broke in the sister at this point. 'You've had quite a busy time, haven't you Harry? First your nephew, then your niece.'

'Aye, sister, it's been quite a break.' To Janet he said, 'Look after yourself and thanks for coming to see an old chap like me. Come again when you can.'

She promised she would. Outside the ward the sister beckoned her over.

'You seem to have cheered him up a bit,' she admitted grudgingly, 'but I hope he didn't upset you with any of his old tales?'

'What tales?'

'Well, he has fantasies he was poisoned by some mystery germ or something made by the government. It's not unusual. We have people in here who think they are being pursued by foreign agents, or that all their neighbours are in a plot to kill them, that kind of thing.'

'No, no, he didn't say anything like that. We just chatted about this and that, the football season, that kind of thing.'

'Oh well, so long as you know. Will we be seeing you again?'

'I think so. Yes, almost certainly, yes.'

Janet had much to mull over as she drove back to her home. It was all beginning to come together in a very unpleasant way and she could have kicked herself for not searching Charlie's flat more thoroughly.

There was no question of going back to the flat again. She could not believe her luck would hold out twice. Time, however, was running out; her children would be back on the Sunday, and by Monday she had to be back at work.

Casting around for advice, she remembered a friend from university days who had graduated in biochemistry. He had done very well and was now a doctor of biochemistry in a north country polytechnic. They had kept in touch over the years, and it occurred to her that this was something he might know about.

In the early evening she rang him. His wife, after a brief chat about the family, told her that Mark was working late at the college, and gave her the number and extension if it was urgent.

He answered the phone himself. He was working on his own, he said, as it was the only way he could get through the marking. If he took it home, the kids made life difficult. It was nice to hear from her after such a long time and was there anything he could do?

'Well, there is actually. Look, we made chemical weapons didn't we? Before and after the war?'

'Yes, well we did a lot of experimental work and we made the stuff too, for quite a long time.'

'Where?'

'Well a lot of the research was done at Porton Down, that's where they work on that kind of thing. Then they did some more down in Cornwall. Some of the stuff was actually manufactured down there I think. There were probably other places too, but they kept pretty quiet about it all.'

'What kind of chemicals were they?'

'They were mainly based on the organo-chlorines and organo-phosphors – very nasty. What most of today's pesticides are derived from, in fact, which is something in my field. Why do you want to know?'

34

'It's a bit difficult to explain. I'll write about why, but do you think you could give me some more details over the phone. The post is so awful.'

'Look,' he said, 'this must cost you a fortune. Let me work out a few facts for you and I'll ring you back in a few minutes.'

When the phone rang again, she was sitting by it with a note-book and pen.

'Right, now, the compounds attack the stuff at the nerve ends, cholinesterase it's called. *That* controls your muscles, so they don't work properly, they can't relax. So your whole body goes into spasms.'

'If you got heavily contaminated with one, what would happen?'

'You'd die. If it was very severe, it would only take minutes. Your heart, lungs and blood pressure would be affected, your whole respiratory system would stop working, and you'd die. If the dose wasn't quite so high but still lethal, you'd probably die over the next day or two.'

'What if it wasn't quite so severe?'

'Then you'd end up pretty sick. You'd have all the symptoms I've described but less severely and you'd spend the rest of your days having all kinds of attacks of dizziness and so on and you'd probably have bad muscular control. It attacks the whole nervous system, you see.'

'If you did die of it, would anybody know?'

'Well, obviously, if you'd been actually handling it at the time. Otherwise it would be very difficult to diagnose. Any doctor would need to know what to look for; there's a special blood test they can do at Porton Down if the blood is fresh.'

'Could they tell if anyone alive had been contaminated?'

'Again, if they knew what to look for, there are certain tests they could do at Porton. But they'd know it was a possibility if they could see your nervous system was shattered and that you twitched. Over the years you would almost certainly develop heart and lung trouble and there might be some residue in your liver.'

'But you wouldn't go mad?'

'No, although you might get periods of confusion. Hey, what is this? You writing a treatise or something?'

'It's more "something" actually. Thanks very much indeed. I'll write and tell you what I needed to know. I might need some more help.' Replacing the receiver, she went to her typewriter and wrote a careful, unemotional account of what she had discovered so far and took it across the road to catch the early morning post.

On the way back she decided to go for a drink. The landlord of the Blue Lion was deep in conversation with a red-faced man in a raincoat, who was methodically drinking scotch.

'Here she is,' said the landlord. 'Hello, my dear. I was just telling this gentleman from the newspapers that you were a friend of Charlie Spencer's.'

'Here, let me buy you a drink. The name's Bill Baxter. I work for the *Clarion*.'

She accepted his offer warily.

'The landlord tells me you were a mate of the young chap that died?'

'That's right. He used to pop in at the library where I work and we had the odd drink and meal together, nothing more. Why do you want to know?'

'Just a matter of interest. Let's have a seat over there.'

He led her to a quiet corner and continued. 'I expect you're upset about the business. What did you think of his dying so suddenly?'

'What do you expect me to tell you?'

'Now come on, don't be so suspicious. He used to do a bit of work for us from time to time, and we were interested in the story, since no one seems to know how he died. I mean it's a bit odd, isn't it? Healthy young chappy like that, found on a deserted beach on Monday morning, stone dead, not drowned. The landlord says you were in here with him on the Friday night?'

She cursed the small-time village life, which meant that her every move was monitored.

'Ye-es, well, we had a drink and a curry.'

'Did he tell you what he was working on?'

She was taken aback, and even more suspicious. Baxter persisted: 'You see he rang me on Saturday to say he was on to a good story. I dropped in at the *Bugle*, casual like, just saying I used to know him in London, and the news editor looked up the schedule for last week. He'd done a break-in at a garage, a couple of council committee meetings, and on the Saturday lunchtime he was going to cover a speech by some junior minister who was opening an old people's home. Hardly the stuff that would make the *Clarion* hold its front page. So it couldn't have been anything the *Bugle* knew about.'

She still couldn't bring herself to say much.

'Well, he did say to me he felt he was on to a good story and that it might make the nationals,' she told him cautiously.

'Nothing more than that?'

'N-no.'

He looked at her shrewdly. 'Look, if you change your mind I'll be staying at the Bell for a couple of days. Another drink?' She declined and, pleading tiredness, went back home.

Part of her wanted to tell the journalist all she knew and let him get on with it. The other part felt she would be better keeping quiet and seeing how much further she could get on her own.

Harry's story was convincing but it would need checking out. She would have to try to find out more from the families of the other survivors. It would depend heavily on what they could remember. But would Charlie's poking into a story at least fifteen years old, however unpleasant, be dangerous enough for somebody to decide he shouldn't continue with it? On the face of it, the idea seemed ridiculous, but it was always possible that even at this distance in time, a story of that sort could prove at the very least embarrassing.

She decided she would give it another day and then hand over everything she had discovered to Inspector Latimer. He had seemed sympathetic and intelligent. Possibly, too, she might then mention her suspicions to Baxter. After which, she could get on again with her own life.

7.

The next morning she took the bit between her teeth and sought out Pete Burrows's widow. A pleasant-looking, middle-aged woman opened the door to her.

'Forgive me for troubling you like this, but I wanted to ask you something about Harry Wharton.'

'You'd better come in.'

She was ushered into a sitting-room, so clean and tidy it made her feel guilty once again over the cluttered mess at home.

'What do you want to know?' asked the woman.

'It's difficult for me to explain. You see, I was a friend of the young man who was found dead on the beach at Shingle Street. He told me before he died that he'd been to see Harry Wharton, so I went to see him too, and he told me a very strange story. He told me he and your husband and two other men were working up at a Ministry place at Shingle Street and that he thought there was some kind of accident which was hushed up, but which made him ill and killed your husband.'

'You'd better sit down,' said Mrs Burrows, 'and I'll make some tea.'

She explained to the widow that she had no right at all to be there asking questions and she would quite understand if Mrs Burrows felt unable to answer them or told her to mind her own business.

'No, I don't think that, though it seems funny after all this time. I never was satisfied but I never got anywhere. You see Pete was real fit, he played football every spare minute he could. The kids were little and he'd play with them too, for hours. He was a real open air man.' Her face softened. 'Like a big kid he was, always showing how fit he was. After he went to that place, he came home real queer with a terrible headache. That wasn't a bit like him. He sat in that chair all night and I even had to turn the telly off – he said it hurt his head.

'Then in the morning he got really bad. He was gasping for breath, and a funny colour and that sick . . . he couldn't stop vomiting. Of course I got in the doctor and they took him off to the hospital and then they rang me to say he was being rushed up to London.'

'Did they say what it was?'

'They didn't tell me anything, except that he was very ill. I ran about like a mad thing, our Freda was only eight months old and the other two were only three and four, and I had to get them all looked after. And then they told me he wasn't going to London after all but to a military hospital in St Albans. The next day I went up there. It took two trains, and when I got there the doctor took me in a little room and told me Pete was dead. Just like that. I asked why he was in that hospital but they just said there were experts there. They said he died of a massive heart attack.'

She looked through one of the drawers in her gleaming sideboard. 'Here's the death certificate.'

It said 'heart failure'.

Janet thanked her and, carefully remembering the date of death, took her leave.

'If you can find anything out let me know,' said the other woman. 'I never found another man like Pete. He was a one-off. The kids can hardly remember him. If I'd had time and money I'd have found out what was the matter. It must have been something funny, or why did the other two die as well?'

Sitting back in the car, Janet felt she was in such deep water that it was in danger of closing over her head. She decided on her return to call in on Latimer at police headquarters, but first she would go to Shingle Street.

A series of confusing lanes led her to a road that ran beside one of the American air bases. 'Now that really does look sinister,' she thought, as she saw the ranks of bunkers, the floodlights, the high wire and the guarded gates. More lanes took her on to a road marked with a T-junction sign, and this soon dwindled to a made-up track which crossed scrub and marshland, finally petering out below a ridge of sand and pebbles and a cluster of houses. They were strung out in a row. The place seemed almost deserted. She walked along the front of the row. Some were empty and awaiting holidaymakers, and there was also a newish-looking hall of some kind, presumably the one about which she had been told. There was little sign of life there either.

Along the beach, sorting out gear for a boat, was a swarthy man in a cap. She passed him and stood at the edge of the water on a spit of sand. There was nothing to see. The tide was out, leaving an expanse of pebbles and a line of seaweed and rubbish.

On her way back she said hello to the boatman.

'I found a body just where you were standing. It was on Monday,' he told her importantly.

'Oh really! The young man that was drowned?'

'That's him. Funny business. He wasn't drowned, they say, though. Thought it was funny at the time. They don't usually come in here if they've fallen out of a boat. The tide usually takes them further on, past the point.' She made a non-committal noise, and he went back to his work.

On her way home she bought the *Bugle*. It gave a short report, on page one, of the opening of the inquest on Charles Spencer. There was a brief account of how the body had been found. The police doctor had said he could find no evidence of foul play. The father had identified the body as that of his son. And the inquest had been adjourned for a fortnight, following a request from the police that they should make further inquiries. That was all.

Keeping to her decision, she went once more to Stembridge police headquarters and asked for Inspector Latimer.

When she saw him again she was very apologetic.

'Look, I'm very sorry to trouble you but you did say to come back if I thought I had any more information.'

'And you think you have?'

'Yes. You know I told you he was talking about Shingle Street. Well, I think he had stumbled across a story about some kind of an accident that took place there – not during the war, but a few years ago.'

'And you think this might have some bearing on his death?'

'I honestly don't know.' She wondered whether or not to mention how far she had taken her own investigations and then decided against it. The inspector did not seem very interested in what she had to say. 'I think he had started making inquiries in the neighbourhood and I think he might have gone up there on that Saturday night. That's all. But I thought you might like to know.'

'Well, thank you again, Mrs Simms. I'll bear it in mind, but we are actually pursuing our own line of inquiry. All I can say at this stage is that it concerns his personal, not his professional, life and I must emphasise that there is no reason anyway to think he met his death other than by accident.'

After he had shown her out, he began to wonder if, after all, she wasn't rather neurotic. Perhaps she hadn't enough to occupy her since Spencer's death and that is why it was preying on her mind so much. He sighed; two women, both concerned in their own ways and both over a young man who, he was inclined to feel, was not worthy of anybody's trouble. The picture of Spencer building up was not a pleasant one.

He supposed he would have to face tackling Stimpson but felt daunted: how best to do it? He called Chapman in and they discussed what their next move would be.

'I've had that woman in again, Mrs Simms. She's really got some bee in her bonnet now that Spencer was working on some investigative story and making inquiries about goings-on at Shingle Street. She seemed so sensible too, but I'm really beginning to think she's one of those people who read something sinister into anything to do with officialdom.'

'Did she say what she had in mind?'

'Something to do with an accident there, a few years ago, when some of the old buildings were still in use.'

'I never heard anything, if there was.'

'Nor me. I imagine it's got something to do with the original scare story from up there, retold with embellishments. You know how these things get garbled.'

He then applied himself to a pile of paperwork. Sometimes he felt that most police time nowadays consisted of handing out and receiving bits of paper.

41

He had specifically asked that he should not be disturbed and, when he was told he had another visitor, he said quite sharply that he could see nobody.

As he spoke, however, a tall elderly man slipped quietly past the constable in the doorway and into the room. He wore a neat, dark suit and carried a briefcase.

'I must apologise for bothering you when you are obviously so busy,' he said smoothly, 'but I'm afraid what I have to say won't wait. My name's Chalmers. I'm from the Ministry of Defence.'

8.

One of Janet's small extravagances was Eileen. Eileen came in and 'did' a couple of days a week, usually while Janet was out. If Janet was in, she was treated to the dramas with which Eileen's life was surrounded – her old man, her children (six of them), *their* problems, her rows with her neighbours. In her mind, Eileen lived out a perpetual soap opera in which she starred, and each visit would culminate in some cliff-hanger that Eileen had to resolve.

Janet was much amused, and when she was at home provided a sympathetic listener. She had helped Eileen to fill in forms, for whatever purpose, and had helped her when she needed advice.

It was not unusual, therefore, for her to arrive home and find Eileen in a state of wild excitement with some pressing drama to tell. This time, however, was different. As she returned, deflated, from seeing Latimer, and entered her own house, she began to think once again that the whole affair really was no concern of hers, she should leave it alone. It was likely that both she and Charlie had been carried away by the idea of some kind of cover up.

She looked into her sitting-room in astonishment. Books, of which there were plenty, had been pulled out of their shelves and were lying in heaps; the papers on her desk, which stood under the window at one end of the room, were mixed together in a pile. In the middle of the room Eileen sat on a chair, clutching a cup of tea and pink with excitement.

'Good God. Whatever has happened?'

'It were the police, Mrs Simms.'

'The police! It couldn't have been. I've just this minute come from police headquarters myself. They would surely have told me. Now tell me exactly what happened and who you let in.'

Eileen was only too delighted. This was the kind of situation she loved.

'Well, I was cleaning up in the kitchen when the bell rang and there were two young men on the step. They asked if you was in and I said you wasn't and they asked if you was at work then, and I said no, I thought you'd gone off somewhere for the day.

'So one of them says, well, we're police officers and we've got to come in and look around. I says, ho ho, yes, I don't believe you, and he gets out a little plastic card thing and it has his name on it, sergeant something-or-other, and he says do you want to see my warrant too, and then pushes past. Next thing I know he's tipping out all your books. I says to him, here, you can't do that, and he says we can do what we damn well like.'

'Did they take anything away?'

'No. I stood here all the time and I said Mrs Simms'll be real mad when she gets back, and you takes something away over my dead body . . .' She finished on a note of high satisfaction.

'Did they say anything else? That they'd be back?'

'No, they didn't say nothing else. They just got mad when they couldn't find what they wanted and then left.'

'Thanks, Eileen. Make us both another cup of tea while I ring the police.'

Latimer and Chalmers were deep in conversation when Sergeant Chapman knocked on the door.

'I've got your Mrs Simms on the phone.'

'Well, you can see I can't be bothered with it now. Tell her to ring back.'

'I don't think that will do, sir. She's furious. She wants to know why our men went and turned her house over while she was out today.'

'The woman's mad! All right, I'll take the call.' He excused himself to Chalmers.

At her end of the line Janet poured out her fury at how she had been treated. Latimer heard her in silence, then said, 'Look, Mrs Simms, whatever idea you might have got into your head, none of my men visited your home this afternoon. I would have had to authorise such a visit, and I would have needed proof that you were likely to be involved in something of a serious criminal nature to even contemplate such a procedure.'

She was not convinced.

'No, I don't disbelieve you. Obviously your cleaning lady has had a fright and it is evident that somebody came to your home and passed himself off as a policeman. You should warn anybody working for you to demand proof of identification. That's how burglaries are committed – people pretend to be policemen, meter readers and so on.'

'But,' said Janet, 'this man did have some kind of police identification. Mrs Margerum, my cleaning lady, said one of them was a sergeant.'

'All I can reiterate, Mrs Simms, is that nobody was involved from my force. If you wish to enter a formal complaint, then my desk sergeant will be available to take it down.'

He replaced the receiver. 'Sorry about that.'

His visitor shifted uneasily.

'Er . . .' he said, 'was that a Mrs Janet Simms, from White House Cottages, River Lane?'

'Yes,' replied Latimer in some surprise.

'Well, it could just be that she's right.'

'But I know none of my men were involved in a house search of that nature – and a pretty unintelligent one, too, by the sound of it.'

'No, I know they weren't. I imagine the visitors were from the Special Branch.'

'What the hell are they doing on my patch?'

'That's what I'm here for. Mrs Simms has been looking into the death of a Mr Charles Spencer, found on a beach here last Monday.'

'Yes. She's come into us twice. She was a close friend of his. But if you look through his file you'll see, first, that we can find no obvious cause of death, no confirmation of foul play, and that secondly, he was mixed up with a local, wealthy, married woman, married to an eminently respectable but unpleasant prominent citizen. We are about to interview the gentleman concerned and I can tell you I'm not looking forward to it. He happens to be a JP sitting on our local bench.'

'By all means carry on with your inquiries. In fact I think it would help. Spencer, you see, had become involved in a very serious matter.'

Eileen had finally been sent off, clutching her money and obviously unable to wait to get home and tell the neighbours and her family about Mrs Simms's strange visitors. Janet sipped a tepid cup of tea, and felt a cold, sick feeling spreading through her. If her visitors were not from the local police, then where were they from? She had no reason to believe that Latimer was lying.

It must have something to do with Charlie's death. It had to be that. Nothing else could explain it.

Her life was pleasant, if unexciting. She had already had enough of London when the chance came to move out. She had a pretty, comfortable, if untidy home. The children – when not yearning for city life – had settled down well in their new schools and had already found friends. She had a reasonable social life; the library was a good place through which to meet people. Her one previous excursion into detection had been very satisfying, but she had intended to leave it at that.

She thought far into the night about whether or not to hand over all she knew to that journalist, Baxter, and then leave it to him. But how strong was his newspaper about actually using material like that, even if it was given to them? Its campaigning issues were usually of a simple and uncontroversial kind.

Sleepless at 2 a.m., she made a cup of tea and reluctantly took a sleeping pill, something she rarely did, and fell into a heavy sleep.

She was woken by the telephone ringing away in the hall. As she stumbled down to answer it, she saw it was nine o'clock.

It was her friend Mark ringing from his college.

'Good heavens, were you still in bed?'

She yawned and said she had had a bad night.

'I'm not surprised,' he replied. 'I've just read your letter. For God's sake have you any idea just what you might be getting into?'

She said that that was what had kept her awake half the night.

He continued: 'What you are saying is that there was some kind of a plant down there that experimented with nerve gases and that there was some kind of accident during the war that was hushed up. On top of that, there was another mishap some time ago as a result of which three people died and one was made so ill that the MoD were able to get him sectioned as crazy.'

'That's right.'

'And you think that had something to do with your friend's death?'

'It must have. It can't have been just a coincidence.'

There was a pause.

'Look,' she asked him, 'are there any books I could read on the subject? And what would they do with any stuff they had made?'

'I can give you a list of books, though how many would make any sense to you I don't know. As to the stuff they made – well, so far as I know only Porton now does the research. They closed down Nancekuke in Cornwall. I imagine they must have some of the stuff stored away in containers somewhere in liquid form. It would keep quite well. That's what makes the pesticides based on these things a problem – the residue of some of them can hang around for a long time even when they're exposed to air.'

'Going back to Harry,' she said, 'he did say all the pipes seemed clear.'

'That might well be. You can't smell it, taste it or even see it. There could have been a minute drop at the bottom of the trap of the sink. That's all it would have taken to do all that damage.'

'Slowly the poison the whole bloodstream fills . . .'

'What?'

'A poem – Empson. It goes on: "the waste remains, the waste remains and kills." '

'Listen, love,' he said, finally, 'think hard before you do any more on this. And another thing – if you want to ring me again don't ring from your home to mine. Ring me here from a call box and I'll ring you back.'

'What on earth for?'

'Because, my dear, you just might find your phone has been put on a tap, and someone has forgotten to get around to informing the Home Secretary.'

She had two clear days left.

She decided to have one more look at Shingle Street itself and then contact Baxter at the Bell – if he was still there – and tell him all she knew.

It was raining when she took the turning down to Shingle Street. The place was deserted. She walked up and down the beach, slipping and sliding on the shingle, into a strong head wind. A solitary fisherman, muffled like an eskimo, was standing on the beach, fishing with a sea rod. Leaving her car near the beach, she walked back along the lane through which she had driven.

At the side of the road was a scrubby piece of woodland and an area of marsh. An old metal gate, very rusty, was wired up with fairly new barbed wire, and there was more barbed wire on the inside of the thickish hedge that bordered the wood. On her way back along the hedge, she found a spot where there was a very small gap. With great difficulty she squeezed through it and found that the barbed wire had been neatly clipped through.

She pushed on through a mass of wet undergrowth, marshy grass and brambles and came upon a rough pathway where the flowers and nettles had been trodden down. Following the path to its end she found more wire, this time rusted link fencing, around some kind of compound. Every few feet there were faded notices saying 'Ministry of Defence – Keep Out'. There was no sign of life. Brambles grew up against the fence in most places, but after half an hour's search she found a small place where it was possible to get through them and where the wire fencing had come loose from its stakes. She crawled underneath.

Most of the buildings that had stood there had long been demolished. Only the brick foundations remained, and the concrete floors. Elder and nettles were pushing up through the concrete, and the brambles and small shrubs covered most of the foundations. There was, however, one hut intact. Its windows were covered in dirt and looked little used, but it did have an oiled double-padlock on the door. A little further on, she came to some overgrown underground bunkers, similar to those at the air base but smaller. They too looked deserted, but they had very heavy metal doors, and there was no apparent way of opening them.

She walked back to the hut and this time went around it completely. One of the dirty windows at the back had been broken and temporarily repaired. Several new thick pieces of wood had been nailed across the opening. She decided to return at a less conspicuous time.

She retraced her journey uneventfully, recovered her car and drove home. On the way she decided that she would contact Baxter and tell him all she knew. At the very least it would be another pair of feet to cover the ground. Time was running out.

She called in at the Bell just before lunchtime. Yes, Mr Baxter was still staying on, but he had gone out for the day. No, he had left no message. She left a note to say she had called and that she would come back mid evening.

When she returned, he was waiting for her. He bought her a drink and took a good look at her.

'You've got something to tell me?'

She nodded and looked around the crowded bar area.

He took her point. 'Have you eaten? No? Good. Then come and have something to eat.'

'You are,' she said, as they sat down, 'probably going to think I'm mad. But I've decided that the time has come when I must talk to somebody else.'

He nodded. 'I've been doing a bit of poking around on my own account,' he told her. 'I imagine Charlie found out that there was some kind of an accident at Shingle Street during the war and that he thought he was on to what it was. I've been on to our people back at the office, and so far no one's come up with anything. I've tried people locally down here, but nobody seems to know, except that it was something nasty.'

During the course of a meal she hardly tasted, she took him, step by step, through what she had found out. She also told him what her friend Mark had passed on about chemical agents and about her visit to Shingle Street and the disused complex behind the wire. Finally she told him about her visit from the Special Branch.

He heard her out in silence, except for the odd, shrewd question.

In the lounge, over coffee, he made a number of careful, methodical notes.

'I can't promise what the *Clarion* will do with this – if anything. The editor's not noted for sticking his neck out on this kind of story. But I'll have a word with the news editor and stay on for a bit.' She told him she would have to be back at work on the Monday.

'I think you and I might usefully go back to Shingle Street soon and see what else we can find, at a time when we're unlikely to be noticed. In the meantime, I'll get our blokes back in the office to see what they can find out about nerve gas plants. And first thing Monday, I'll get someone to go to St Catherine's House and get a copy of Burrows's death certificate.'

'It said heart failure.'

'So you said, but it's worth another look. No wonder Charlie thought he was on to something. But if he was, then actually to go as far as killing him seems a bit extreme, even if he was looking into things he shouldn't. He went about it quite wrongly, of course,' he said. 'Ideally you should get the full backing of your editor behind you when you start on something like this. And the legal boys. If you just can't, then at least you must make sure one other person knows exactly where you are and what you are doing and is kept informed. It's madness just to rush at it solo.'

'That was Charlie all over. He'd had trouble before on a story where he insisted on doing it this way.'

'You've been very persistent. What put you on to it in the first place?'

'It sounds stupid but just an intuition really. Right from the start, the whole thing didn't sound right. His lonely death, the way people reacted. I just felt that this time he might well have been on to something. That's why I went to the police.'

'I don't think that's stupid at all. It's what a journalist would call a "nose", that hunch you can't explain which means you know you're on to a good story in the teeth of all the evidence. It's what makes a good journalist rather than a competent one. I think we should go back to St Leonard's tomorrow and see your man Harry.'

'I'm glad I decided to tell you. At least somebody else knows now and doesn't think I'm neurotic. Especially after the visit I had today.'

'That was very nasty – and crass with it. I imagine it was designed more to frighten you off than to actually try to discover something. I think you've stumbled across something pretty unpleasant. I don't like to think of that poor bloke stuck in a funny farm through no fault of his own, but just because it's convenient for the Ministry of Defence. I don't like to hear about journalists who meet unexplained deaths while they're working on embarrassing stories. And I don't like big-headed Special Branch cops trying out their macho on women.'

She felt immensely relieved.

'Look,' he continued, 'take the morning off from it all, go for a walk, read a book, do whatever you do. I'll follow up the families of the other two men involved. It might add something to what we already know, and I'll let you know what I find out when I see you tomorrow afternoon to go up to the hospital.

9.

When she reached home she found that, late as it was, she had a visitor. A pasty-faced man with cropped hair, in his mid-thirties she reckoned, was standing on her doorstep peering through the letter box.

'Can I help you?' she asked.

'Are you Mrs Simms? Mrs Janet Simms?'

'That's right.'

'My name's Colmore and I would like to ask you a few questions.'

'Who are you? Where are you from?'

'Special Branch, Detective-Sergeant Colmore.' Seeing her reaction, he wearily reached inside his jacket and produced his warrant card.

'Well,' she said, 'I suppose you'd better come in, although I imagine you've already been in once today. I can't imagine what it is you want to talk to me about.'

She deliberately did not ask him to sit down but left him standing, running his warrant card up and down between his fingers as he stared at her. Then he sat down without invitation.

'So you thought you'd help the police with their inquiries?'

'Oh, you mean by calling in about Charlie?'

'That's right. It seems you told Inspector Latimer you thought your young friend was on to some kind of a scoop?'

'Well, perhaps not as dramatic as that. I told them that he thought he was on to a good story. I also said that I seemed to recollect he had mentioned Shingle Street and that was why I thought it odd when his body was found there.'

'Why?'

'Well, it is odd, isn't it? Nobody has yet come up with any explanation of why he died.'

'Why do you think he died?'

'Good heavens, how should I know? I merely found it odd, that's all. That's why I decided to call in on the police after I had seen the inquest report. I thought it might help.'

He hardly seemed to be listening. He was looking along her crowded bookcases. 'Interested in politics, are you?'

There were some books on political issues, various others on conservation and nuclear power, far more on Elizabethan drama and shelves of novels.

'Along with many other things.'

'Take part in demos and all that kind of thing?'

'I can't see that's got anything to do with you or anything else,' she said, getting up and very obviously waiting for him to leave.

'Been down to Shingle Street, have you?'

She hesitated. 'Once or twice I suppose, over the last twelve months.' She was strictly truthful.

'May I give you some advice?'

'If you like.'

'Don't waste anybody's time any more. Work in the library, don't you? I think you've been reading too many romances, too many murder stories in the quiet times. You seem to have made quite a little fantasy out of it with your mysterious stories and unexplained deaths.'

She was furious. 'I'm not in the habit of inventing fantasies and I wish I had never been near the police station. What I told the police was absolutely true. The night before he died, Charlie Spencer had told me he was on to a good story, and that seemed relevant enough to me. Anyway, if you think I'm indulging in neurotic fantasies, then what the hell are you doing here at this time of night or barging into my house, turning over my books and papers? Don't tell me local corpses are a problem for the Special Branch!'

He stood up, snapping shut his notebook.

'The inquest will resume next week, Mrs Simms. A verdict of death by cause or causes unknown will be returned. And that will be that. End of story. I must ask you to stop persisting with any lines of inquiry you might be considering. They won't lead anywhere and, like I said, you're only wasting your own and everyone else's time.'

As she closed the door behind him, she felt quite shaken.

Latimer was not too happy to be knocked up at home, late in the evening, either. He and his wife were watching the end of a television programme before going to bed. The arrival on his doorstep of Colmore was greeted without enthusiasm.

'Yes,' he said, peremptorily, after Colmore had explained who he was. 'Won't it wait? I'll be in my office, as usual, tomorrow morning.'

'You've spoken to Mr Chalmers from the MoD – sir,' he added as an afterthought. 'I'm sure he will have told you the serious nature of the business we have in hand.'

Latimer regarded him with distrust. 'I suppose you'd better come in.' He looked at Colmore with dislike. Not all ordinary policemen liked the Special Branch. On his side Colmore, like many of his colleagues, regarded the rest of the force as heavy-footed plodders. Out here in the sticks, he thought, they were likely to be particularly thick.

'I don't see how you can expect us to co-operate fully if you can't tell us what it's all about,' remarked Latimer.

'It's all under wraps, that's why. Ministry of Defence chap must have told you that. The most important thing is that we don't get any bungling amateurs messing around where they shouldn't.'

'You saw Mrs Simms then?'

'Yeah – one of these trendy lefties, I suspect. Books on the bomb and all that kind of thing in the sitting-room. Very much on her dignity and I-know-my-rights bit. Still, I think I made it clear that she was wasting everybody's time.'

'What about the journalist Baxter? Have you seen him?'

'Shouldn't think he'd be much trouble. I'll call him in over the weekend and tell him that there's absolutely no point at all in his staying around. He's not been doing much, has he?'

'Not that I know of. But then I haven't had anyone following him around. Whatever he did would be pretty obvious in a place like this anyway.'

'Simms did say the lad had been interested in Shingle Street. Do you think he told her anything else?'

'If he did, she said nothing to us.'

'Anyhow we've had a tap on the line since Tuesday. The miracles of modern science. It's a far cry since chaps like us used to sit in on intercepted calls with a notebook. All done by microchip these days. If she's dreamed up anything difficult and talked to anyone about it, then we'll soon know.'

'I suppose you can't tell me what happened?'

'About Shingle Street? To be honest I don't know what happened there during the war. As to what's happened since, well, it's not for me to say.'

'And Charles Spencer?'

'Now that really is a mystery. He was on to something that took him up there on the Saturday night.'

'So you weren't responsible for what happened?'

'Me, personally? Good God, no. He wasn't killed to stop him talking or anything like that – it's hardly in that league. We're just as mystified as you are.'

'Have you any idea what he died of?'

'Now that is something about which we might have some knowledge. If we could only have got hold of the body before it went in the water, we might well have been able to tell. But if it is what it looks as if it might be, then it's still something of a mystery. It means he had got hold of something he shouldn't have, and we can't find out how or where. Anyway we will, of course, pass on to you anything we might turn up on that one. In the meantime perhaps you can keep tabs on Simms and Baxter in a discreet kind of way.'

'I'll do what I can. From what I've found out, her children are back any time, and she's due back at work in the library Monday morning. She can't do much from there. As to Baxter, I'll have him in and say there are no more developments and he's wasting his time messing around down here. Perhaps your office or the MoD could have a word with his office. Personally, I find the whole thing unpleasant and distasteful. It's not the way I like to work.'

Latimer was becoming increasingly unhappy. He was one of the new breed of senior policemen. National Service had been followed by university and then the police. He had moved up through the ranks steadily, and he knew he was tipped as a possible chief constable. He could be extremely tough – and short-tempered – but he was imaginative and fair. Colmore's way of working was diametrically opposed to his own. Violent crime was comparatively rare in his patch, but he had plenty of contacts and was respected. It was not too difficult, as a rule, to find out what was going on or who had been seen where.

There had been very few murders during his time at Stembridge. There had been little Maureen Daly who, at seventeen, had traded her favours to most of the lads in the locality. She had assured young Brian Gibbs that the baby she was expecting was his, only to inform him shortly after the wedding that it was not. In the resulting monumental quarrel, he had hit her over the head with a heavy lamp base and cracked her skull. Neighbours heard a racket

54

and sent for the police. When Latimer arrived, he found the lad in tears and only too ready to confess.

Then there had been the fight between tinkers camping on the common, a sudden gun fight, and the murderer picked up some twenty miles away with little trouble.

There had, of course, been one or two unexplained corpses. Joshua Martle, found dead in a hedge. He had been the meanest man for miles, an appalling landlord, an amateur money lender and suspected of blackmail. Nobody ever came forward to assist with any information about what he was doing four miles from his home in the middle of nowhere and wearing his carpet slippers. And that had been that.

But Charles Spencer was different. When Latimer had first heard that he had not drowned, he had kept an open mind about what had happened, particularly as there seemed to be no obvious or even possible cause of death. The links with the Stimpsons were interesting, but not necessarily significant.

Chalmers, from the Ministry, had been extremely civil but uncommunicative. In the most courteous way, he had informed Latimer that the Special Branch would also be looking into Spencer's death from now on and that any help the local police might offer would be most welcome. This had prompted Latimer, not surprisingly, to ask just what it was all about.

Chalmers had told him there was very little he could say.

'During the war, as you know, the Ministry had research facilities at Shingle Street. There are still storage areas there. It could be that Mr Spencer was investigating these – which was, of course, reprehensible of him. We do need, therefore, to look into the matter further ourselves.'

Janet got through the morning with ill-concealed impatience. Just before two, Baxter knocked on her door.

'How did you get on?'

'Very well. I've lots to tell you. But let's go and see Harry first. Then I'll fill you in.'

When they arrived she led him through to the dayroom of the ward where she had seen Harry at the beginning of the week. The same sister was on duty at a small office at the end of the corridor.

'It's Mrs Simms again, sister. I've come to see my uncle, Harry Wharton.'

The sister looked blank.

'Really, Mrs Simms. Hasn't Mr Wharton's son been in contact with you?'

'No. Should he have been?'

'It seems a bit strange. Hasn't he told you his uncle has been moved?'

'Moved where?'

'To a nice private home, I understand. His son rang us to say he had agreed for his father to go into a private home and that transport would be sent for him. Two young gentlemen arrived with a note from a new doctor, and Mr Wharton left yesterday. Of course, it's a relief to us. We need all the bed space we can get.'

'Did they say where he'd been taken?'

'I can't say I remember. It was nearer to London, I think. No – no, I don't seem to have made any note of it here. You'll just have to ask his son, won't you?'

Janet and Bill turned and walked back through the corridors and out into the car.

'It appears,' said Bill, 'that nobody is taking any chances.'

'How can we find out where he is?'

'Let me use your phone and I'm pretty sure I can try.'

Back at her house he rang the hospital and asked to be put through to the secretary's office.

'My name's Smith,' he said, 'DHSS in Ipswich. We understand one of your patients, a Mr Wharton, has been moved recently, and his new pension book will need to be sent to his new hospital. Nobody has informed us of the address and we need to sort out the paperwork.'

There was a pause and then Bill started writing it down. 'The Flora Mottingham Home, Deston, near Chelmsford. Thank you very much. Most helpful.' He replaced the receiver.

'How on earth did you get away with that?'

'If someone rings up in an authoritative way and asks for the Secretary's office and says he's Joe Bloggs from the DHSS demanding information, few people bother to question it.'

'Have you done it before, then?'

'Well, similar things from time to time. Otherwise you'd never find anything out.'

'It seems they had a call from Harry's son – and what a louse he must be – saying he'd had a bit of luck and someone had offered to pay for the old chap to go into this private loony bin near Chelmsford. He thanked them for all they'd done for dear old Dad and said the people from the new place would be turning up with the appropriate paperwork to collect him. Make us a cup of coffee, love, and I'll see what I can find out about the Flora Mottingham Home.'

As she made coffee in the kitchen, she could hear him involved in a long discussion. As she came back he replaced the receiver.

'Well, it's all in order. The place does exist. I rang them saying our family was worried about dear old Auntie Violet, charming old thing but a bit off her rocker, and what was the position if I wanted to get her a place? I was informed that the home was up to the very highest standards, with every possible medical and psychiatric facility – full of the best nutters, in fact. She quoted some astronomical price and told me that all the necessary papers would be needed if Auntie Violet had to be put in there, and of course if dear Auntie was accepted and needed help, there was no problem whatsoever.

'I asked about visiting, and the old bird said of course it was "flexible, being a *private* establishment", but the staff preferred the afternoons. I said we'd discuss it among ourselves and let her know about Auntie. It's just on three. I reckon we'd make it up there a little after four. The old boy obviously trusts you – let's go and see him. On the way I'll tell you all I found out this morning.'

10.

Within a few minutes they were in his car on the road to Chelmsford.

'This shouldn't take long,' Bill told her. 'It's a good road all the way and, according to the map, Deston's a couple of miles this side of the town itself.

'Now this morning. I got nowhere with Fenn. The old address Harry gave you was no good. They told me the widow had moved away years ago. I finally tracked her down to a council estate just outside Stembridge, but when I knocked on the door, the occupants said she'd died three years ago and all they knew was that she had a son in Yarmouth who worked on the trawlers. I'll follow that up tomorrow.

'Mrs Giggs was more of a help. She's still living in the same house, not far from Mrs Burrows. I told her I was doing some research on sudden and unexplained deaths, and she said her husband's death had never been explained to her satisfaction. Like Burrows, he'd been whipped away to London, but died in one of the London teaching hospitals. By the time she got up there he was unconscious, on some kind of life-support system, and he died without ever coming to. They told her he'd had a stroke and that's what's on his death certificate, cerebral haemorrhage.

'It took a few weeks for her to find out that the two other men had died too. She said Mary Burrows was too upset to do anything much, what with all those little children. She had been to her doctor and said she wasn't at all happy, but he said it was just one of those things – anyone could have a stroke.

'She'd been to see Mrs Wharton a few times too, and she said Harry's symptoms weren't like any stroke she'd ever seen, nor were her husband's. She thought it was pretty fishy when the Whartons told her "they" wanted to get the old boy "certified". But she got caught up in things, and then old Mrs W had died. She said the son was a lazy sod who never did anything for his parents anyway and was probably glad to take the easy way out.'

'It's good of you to take such an interest, but won't your family be expecting you home soon?'

'Don't worry, I suffer from the occupational hazard of Fleet Street – divorce.'

'I'm sorry.'

'Don't be. I could hardly blame poor old Celia. She never saw me. I didn't go in for much of that to-ing and fro-ing and alibis about working late and being sent away and such. But I did have to go away all the time, and she got bored and lonely and fed up. We have two girls. One's fourteen and the other fifteen. Anyway, Celia found someone who could give her far more attention, and that was that. It's quite amicable. I see the girls regularly. I sold up the house. It was too big, and I have a flat, which suits me.'

'You've always been a journalist?'

'Yes. I was the original starry-eyed recruit – a bit like Charlie, I imagine. Went from school on to a weekly, from there on to a local morning paper, and from there to Fleet Street. I've been on the *Clarion* six years. You get all that Street of Adventure shit out of you quite quickly, of course. It's a jungle world, and I'm glad I'm not in the office much, though that can have its problems, too. You can come back from a job to find someone at your desk and the news that you've been fired. It's an unhealthy life, of course. Too much beer, too much hanging around, too much frantic activity, and all too often your work just ends up on the spike.'

Within an hour they found themselves outside the home. It was set in large grounds, and looked as if it had belonged to some wealthy local family.

'You must continue to say you're his niece,' Bill told her. 'You can say I'm a friend who's given you a lift down here, otherwise you couldn't have made the journey.'

'And when they ask me how I knew he was here?'

'Easy. His son, your cousin I assume, told you, knowing how interested you were in dear old Uncle Harry.'

The only way to tell that the Flora Mottingham Home was not a pleasant country club or house was the neat gate office, where a uniformed attendant sat. Janet approached him and said that she was hoping to see her uncle who had recently been admitted to the home. His name was Harry Wharton. This was a friend who had kindly driven her down from Ipswich.

She was asked to sign the visitors' book, and the man pressed an electronic switch to raise the bar across the gateway.

The foyer of the home was even smarter. It was carpeted from wall to wall in dove grey, with matching, discreet wallpaper. A huge flower arrangement stood in an urn on a well-polished table.

'Can I help you?'

A tall, dignified woman in a spotless suit had appeared from a door at the side.

Again Janet went through her story, adding that the last time she had seen her uncle, during the week, he had asked her for some items, which she had brought with her. She had not, she said, realised he was to be moved.

'I understand it was a sudden decision,' said the woman who introduced herself as the home's secretary, Miss Whittington. 'One moment please.' She pressed a bell, and a young woman in a white overall and cap appeared immediately. 'These are visitors for Mr Wharton. Would you have a word with Matron and then let Mr Wharton know they are here.' Then to Janet and Bill she said, 'Do sit down, we'll only keep you a few minutes.'

The few minutes dragged on to nearly half an hour, by which time both Janet and Bill were getting restless and Bill was staring out of the window at the back of the hall. He saw pleasant gardens and terraces where, no doubt, patients could sit in good weather. Behind the old building they were in, there were three newly built, modern ward blocks.

'Mrs Simms?'

Miss Whittington had returned with a very formidable lady indeed. 'This is our matron, Miss Summers.'

They shook hands.

'I'm afraid you've had a wasted journey, Mrs Simms,' said Miss Summers.

'What do you mean?'

'Your uncle has decided that he does not want to see any visitors.'

'I can't believe it. When I saw him last week, he made me

promise to come again. I even brought him some things he'd asked for . . .'

'I'm very sorry, Mrs Simms. If you leave them with us, we'll make sure he gets them.'

'But there must be some mistake. I'm sure he would like to see me.'

'It seems not. Don't take it too much to heart. People suffering from mental illness, like your uncle, can be very changeable and capricious, you know. They don't mean any harm. He was quite adamant that he did not want to see you or anybody else. And there's no point in upsetting him unnecessarily, is there? I'm sure, from what you have seen, you can be confident he is being well looked after. Do come again,' she said, moving purposefully towards the main door, 'but next time give us a telephone call first so that we can see if he wants to see you.'

'Someone already seems to have thought of that one,' said Bill drily, as the electronic barrier was raised on their way out. 'I wonder what happens next.'

He did not have long to wait. On their return to his hotel, they found a message pinned on the noticeboard for him. It was from his paper, taking him off the story and recalling him to the office.

'Don't look so stricken,' he told Janet cheerfully. 'I'm owed God knows how much time off. I'll ring in tomorrow and tell them I'm taking a few days off. If necessary, I'll say I've gone down with flu. I'm not normally all that altruistic,' he said, looking at her surprised face. 'It's just that I don't like being made a fool of either, and I have a natural distrust of the Special Branch. We'll see how much further we can get. Didn't someone once say that the most important quality for a journalist was ratlike cunning?'

The parcel post had come while she was out, and there was a note from the postman through her door: 'two parcels for you in coalhouse as you were not in'. There was something to be said for living in the country. The first turned out to be an unsolicited catalogue, but the other was from Mark and it contained two books on chemical warfare.

Inside was a note from Mark which said: 'I think I'm probably being irresponsible in sending these. Do take care.'

61

She spent the evening poring over them and gathering more information. She learned that most modern gases were derived from those discovered by the Germans before the war – tabun and sarin gases – and that these had organo-phosphorous bases. Even sarin gas was so deadly that one milligram could be lethal if inhaled, and it could also be ingested through the skin. But there was precious little information on British research, nearly all of which was still classified. Most of the papers quoted in the books were either American or German.

She discovered that there had been a number of incidents in the States involving storage of such gases. Now they were generally stored in their separate constituents over there, to avoid any possible trouble. But were there stores of nerve gas agents in the bunkers near Shingle Street? It would explain the secrecy and the Special Branch involvement, but it did not explain Charlie's death. It seemed unlikely he could have got inside one of the bunkers, short of blowing off one of the steel doors.

Her own efforts would now be severely limited. Her children were due back in the morning, and on the Monday she had to be back in the library.

'I'll move out of the Bell to somewhere more discreet and then contact you,' Bill had said. 'Meanwhile, I'll just keep going. You'd be doing yourself a favour by acting as if you'd given up. Go to the pub at lunchtime for a chat about nothing, meet your kids off the coach, do all the routine things. Try not to worry.'

They clambered off the coach clutching plastic carrier bags, badly packed holdalls and, in the case of the eldest, Robin, some appalling padded earphones. She regarded Robin, who was fourteen, with horror.

'What on earth are those?'

'Aren't they *great*? Granddad bought them for me. You can get Radio 1 and 2 on them and you can listen to them anywhere because nobody can hear but you.'

'It's made him even more boring,' said his younger sister, Emma. 'He just goes around all day with a glazed look on his face and he can't hear a thing you say to him. Anyway, Granny bought me some new gear for my present.'

Janet supposed there was some reason why all young girls chose to dress like off-duty traffic wardens. Nasty little ankle boots with pointed heels made her daughter's legs look unattractive; and the point was emphasised by her deep-purple wool tights. An unattractive, black, sack-like pinafore dress topped this, over which was slung, incongruously, her school coat.

'And whatever has Edward got?' she asked them, looking hopelessly at her younger son. He was a placid and easygoing child but with an obstinate streak. His wants had been simple – an Ipswich Town football strip.

Over a huge meal they told her what they had done all week. They had been to the cinema four times, Granny had taken Emma to the ballet at her own request, and the two boys had gone to the Science Museum. They had been to a great pizza parlour ('Why don't you ever cook pizza at home?'), and on the last night they had all gone to a Chinese restaurant in Soho. 'Gran wouldn't let us look in the shop windows,' said Robin wistfully.

At about the time she was greeting her children, John Latimer was reading a lengthy letter from Terence Stimpson in which he pulled no punches.

He had taken great exception, he said, to hearing about the inspector's visit to his home and the questioning of his wife. As a senior police officer, Inspector Latimer hardly needed to have his attention drawn to the fact that the undersigned was a JP, sitting on the local bench. The need, therefore, to pursue what appeared to be meaningless inquiries to his home could only be due to incompetence. Neither he nor his wife, whom he had questioned closely, had even met the young man in question. He trusted that they would hear no more of the matter. But if, in spite of his warning, the inspector continued to pursue his line of inquiry, then he would take the matter higher up – much higher up. He had friends at both New Scotland Yard and the Home Office, not to mention his own MP.

Reluctantly, Latimer called in his shorthand typist to dictate a suitable reply. Chalmers's view, that he should pursue the Stimpson angle regardless, he found unpleasant. He felt that there was a potentially explosive situation there which would take very little to set off. Whatever his own moral views on the behaviour of Frances Stimpson and her relationship with Spencer might be, her husband's brutal behaviour went some way towards explaining it.

He had just finished dictating the letter when Colmore was shown in, and it was obvious that he was very angry. He had been informed of Harry Wharton's visitors, and had a shrewd idea who they were. The matron of the home had done exactly what she had been told: refused to allow anyone to see the old man and rung the number she had been given if anyone attempted it. She had been told that Harry Wharton was, indeed, suffering from mental illness, but that he had been involved in secret work at some stage in his past and that the Ministry were keeping an eye on him. It had been quite easy to persuade Wharton's son to have his father moved, especially with all expenses paid.

'What can I do for you, then? asked Latimer.

Colmore had something of a dilemma. If he complained too bitterly about the couple's visit to the Mottingham Home, he would have to explain why they were there and who was in it. He did not want to do this, even to the uniformed branch. The briefing he had received was quite explicit. The Ministry did not want any more information to be given than was absolutely essential. Yet he was furious that Harry had been found so soon and so easily.

'I want to know what's happened about Simms and Baxter.'

Latimer looked at him in some surprise. 'I had a word with Baxter's editor yesterday and told him there was nothing doing. He said his office were going to recall him anyway – I take it that was done from your end – and I imagine that he'll go away now since there's no reason for him to stay. Mrs Simms is due back at the library and will be stuck there. I can't see what you're worried about.'

'Well, keep tabs on Baxter, will you. Make sure he checks out and goes. Have you a quiet telephone I can use?'

In a small private office he dialled St Leonard's. As they had no idea that there was anything untoward, he decided to deceive them about who he was and then find out, if he could, if anyone had asked about Harry Wharton.

He was put through to the secretary's office. 'Hello,' he said, 'my name's Brown. I'm ringing from the DHSS in Ipswich about Harry Wharton.'

'Haven't you people got anything better to do?' asked an aggrieved voice on the other end. 'I already spoke to one of your chaps – working overtime he was. Perhaps you'd better ask him what you want to know instead of wasting our time again.'

Almost speechless with rage, Colmore said he was sorry. His colleague did not appear to be in, what information had he been given?

'Why, we told the fellow who asked where old Mr Wharton had gone. He said he needed it to alter his social security book or something . . .' Colmore slammed down the phone, leaving the hospital official at the other end to comment once again on the incivility and stupidity of civil servants.

11.

Although it was less than a week since Janet had last worked in the library, it felt like half a year. She walked through a town which had become familiar to her, but which now seemed unreal. She had got the children off to school and then walked through the market, stopping at the vegetable stall and the fish stall. The market square was crowded. It offered not only the usual kinds of things but the trendy up-market wholefoods and craft goods designed to attract commuters and weekend sailors.

Stembridge tended to flood with strangers at weekends and in the summer. It was not so much a holiday resort itself, but with its marina and yacht basin it attracted large numbers of sailing people who used it as a base. The restored tide-mill on the foreshore also attracted its quota of tourists, although these were usually just passing through the town.

Back in the library, Janet parried questions about her holiday. The head librarian remarked pointedly that he trusted nobody else would be requiring leave, as the library was already short-staffed.

If anyone felt that they had time on their hands, there was work to be done checking stock.

At mid morning Bill arrived. He made no sign that he recognised Janet, but merely handed her a note, with the words, 'Can you get this book for me?' The note said that he had moved out of the Bell to a bed-and-breakfast house in a neighbouring village and asked her to meet him as soon as possible.

'I'll just check, but I don't think I have it in stock,' she told him. 'We could probably order it for you from another library. Are you a resident or a holidaymaker?'

'Just passing through. But I'll be here for a few days . . . Perhaps I could call back about lunchtime?'

'I go to lunch from 12.30 to 1.30.'

'Ah well . . . some other time . . .'

As she left the library at lunchtime, he materialised from the car park at the back.

'I've brought some sandwiches and some beer,' he told her. 'Let's go somewhere quiet.'

She led him down to the river bank, and they found a good spot near the marina. He removed the food from his briefcase, and also a folder in which were some photostats of newspaper cuttings.

'I had a hunch, so I went to the library at the *Bugle*, and they let me go through their back numbers and clippings. Just look at this!'

Dated some three years previously was a report headed, 'Suicide Verdict on Lonely Widow'. Underneath, it stated that the coroner had returned a verdict of suicide on Mrs Eliza Fenn, aged 71. Mrs Fenn had taken an overdose of an analgesic prescribed for arthritic pain.

An earlier report noted the finding of Mrs Fenn's body by a neighbour who had called to see if she wanted any shopping done for her. Receiving no reply and finding the back door left unlocked as usual, she had gone upstairs to find Mrs Fenn dead in bed. By the bed was an empty tablet bottle and a note in Mrs Fenn's neat handwriting. It said that she had had so much worry recently that she could no longer go on. Mrs Fenn's doctor, who had been called in, said he knew of no special problems of a medical nature concerning Mrs Fenn, although she did suffer from arthritis. For this

66

he had prescribed a variety of drugs, including the painkiller.

Mrs Fenn, it emerged, had a son, a fisherman living in Great Yarmouth. He was at sea at the time of his mother's death but his wife had given evidence. Her husband had seen his mother recently and had said she seemed anxious about something, but no, she herself had not been told what it was. Presumably her husband had not considered it to be of vital concern. A post mortem had been carried out on Mrs Fenn and it had shown a lethal amount of the drug in her system. She appeared to have gone to bed and taken an overdose some time during the late evening before she was found.

'So I went back to the council estate and knocked up the neighbour whose name and address were given at the inquest. She's one of those nosy-looking women you feel spend all their time squinting from behind their lace curtains. She was a bit surprised when I asked her if I could have a chat about old Mrs Fenn. But she couldn't resist a gossip and so she asked me in.'

Over tremendously strong and sweet tea Mrs Phillips had regaled him with her account of her discovering the body. 'Gave me a real nasty turn. The old girl was a bit feeble on her legs – that's why I did a bit of shopping for her when I went up to town – but she'd not been ill nor nothing. Why do you want to know?'

Bill told her he was researching a book on suicides, and 'a friend' had mentioned Mrs Fenn's death as something of a mystery.

'Well, I wouldn't put it like that,' said Mrs Phillips, settling back in her chair. 'I mean there wasn't nothing fishy discovered at the inquest, if that's what you mean, though nobody knew why she should have done it. But then old people do get queer fancies, don't they?'

'I suppose you knew her well?'

'As well as anyone did. She was always a very quiet little body. Kept herself to herself, didn't mix much, never had. She was like that ever since I knew her, but it got worse after her poor husband died so sudden.'

Bill asked if she had many visitors.

'Well, her son always came regular, I'll give him that. When he was at sea, then his wife used to pop over, and sometimes they all came together, husband, wife and the two grandchildren. No, I can't say I recollect she had many other callers, though there was the two men in a big posh car. They came twice, not long before she died. I thought they must be from the insurance or something. Anyway, they had a big black car and they stayed quite a while the second time they were here.'

'I realise,' Bill told Janet, 'that it's easy to see anything in a sinister light now, however accidental. But I thought you and I might take a run up to Great Yarmouth the first morning you have off and see what we can find out, if anything, from the Fenns.'

'I could probably switch shifts tomorrow. Elaine at the library was grumbling about working tomorrow evening.'

'There's this, too.' He handed her a note. It said that the death certificate for Peter Burrows was at St Catherine's House. It noted that he had died in Rawston Military Hospital, St Albans. Cause of death was given as 'organic poisoning'.

'But that's not what Mrs Burrows's death certificate said!'

'Indeed it did not. Sounds,' said Bill, 'like a case for someone to answer.'

That same lunchtime, Latimer called round at the Bell. No, he told the landlord, thanking him for his offer of a drink; he was on duty. But he would have a ploughman's lunch and a cup of coffee. Oh, and by the way, had a journalist called Bill Baxter checked out?

Yes, the landlord told him. Mr Baxter had checked out that very morning, saying that he had been recalled to London. He was sorry to see him go. The chap had been lavish on the hospitality, had liked his nosh and been quite entertaining in the bar. Not that he'd been in all that much. Baxter might have been working on some story but had not said anything about it.

So that, thought Latimer, is that.

Back at the office, however, he was to receive two disturbing telephone calls within minutes of each other. The first was from Terence Stimpson.

'I'm through to Chief Inspector Latimer then? Did you or did you not receive my letter?'

'Indeed I did – and replied to it.'

'I had your reply. Can you tell me, therefore, why your men are still pestering me and my wife?'

'My men are not pursuing any further inquiries with either of you.'

'Don't try and lie to me, Latimer. You're not dealing with some local poacher. Your men have been found poking around my house twice within the last forty-eight hours, and one of them spent over an hour with my wife. I told you what I would do if this continued. I'm getting straight on to New Scotland Yard.'

'Mr Stimpson, I can assure you – whatever you might think of my integrity – that nobody from my force has been anywhere near your property nor have they spoken to your wife. I'm prepared to swear to that.'

'You may well need to,' shouted Stimpson and slammed down his telephone.

The second call was from Colmore. It was to tell him that Baxter had not returned to his office and had told his editor he was taking a few days' leave.

'I can't help that,' said Latimer. 'He certainly checked out of the Bell this morning and told the landlord that he was going back to London. As far as I'm concerned, he's gone. One of my boys saw his car turning on to the A12 and setting off as if he was going to London. He was doing a fair speed.'

'He might well,' said Colmore sourly, 'but he never reached there. You'd better get one of your chaps to keep an eye out for his car. And if he's still down here, let me know. If he won't do as he's told, then that's his problem.'

'Can I ask what you mean by that?'

'You can ask . . .'

'I dislike pulling rank, Sergeant, but may I remind you that I am actually very much your senior. If I have any more behaviour of this kind, I shall go straight over your head to your superior and if necessary over their head to whoever is pulling the strings. And while we're on the subject, may I ask if you've been poking around Frances and Terence Stimpson's house and questioning the lady? You know very well we've decided that it has nothing to do with Spencer's death now.'

'I thought it would be useful, that's all.'

'Why?'

'I'd have thought it was obvious. It distracts attention from other areas, doesn't it?'

'Then I must order you to stop. The situation there is an extremely difficult one. I don't just mean that the old man has friends in high places. Any further action could trigger off an extremely nasty situation. There's no point whatsoever in your carrying on with this.'

'I'll bear it in mind – sir,' said Colmore and replaced his receiver.

The next morning Bill and Janet were searching through Great Yarmouth, looking for Croft Road and the Fenns. They had decided to be reasonably frank and say that they were newspaper people, investigating a possible accident at Shingle Street some fifteen years before.

They were in luck. Michael Fenn was home from sea. He seemed very doubtful at first but finally agreed to talk a little about his father's death.

'When Dad died, we did assume it was just one of those things. He was pushing sixty and still working hard and people can just die suddenly, can't they? I thought it a bit funny, mind you, when I found out afterwards that two other chaps who worked with him had died around the same time – especially Pete Burrows, who was such a healthy bloke. But with one thing and another I didn't do much about it. I wasn't married then and I was away at sea a lot of the time on the big trawlers – Iceland and so on. I made sure me Mum was all right, mind you. I always sent her a bit on top of her widow's pension and still did, right up until she died, and the wife and I kept an eye on her.'

'We were real cut up when she died like that. It didn't seem right. There was no real reason for it, not that I could see.'

'At the inquest it was said she'd been very worried,' Janet prompted.

'Well,' he looked a bit embarrassed, 'there was something, but it did seem a bit daft to me. It seemed she'd thought about Dad's death a lot during the last months of her life, and finally she went to see old Harry Wharton who worked with Dad on the last job he did. She was a bit surprised to find he'd been put in the big mental home, St Leonard's, and that his wife had died, but she got a bus and went up there to see him.

'It seems he told her some tale about having been contaminated with some germ or something, working up at Shingle Street, and that he'd been put away to keep him quiet.

'Now Mum was an independent old stick, if quiet, and she sat down and wrote to the Ministry in London, saying she didn't think it right old Harry should have been put away like that. She said that her husband had died after working on the same job as Harry and that so had two other men, both of them quite young.

'She said she'd thought about it and thought that something wasn't adding up, and had there been some kind of an accident with some germs or something? If so, then surely she should have had some compensation? Well she didn't hear anything for a while. Then, she said, one day a big car arrived and two fellows in suits got out and asked if they could talk to her about the letter she had written to the Ministry in London.

'They were quite polite, she said, but told her she really mustn't go around saying things like that. The Ministry of Defence was only one lot of people the firm worked for, and sad as it was that three men had died, there was nothing to say that they had died because they had all been working together on one particular day.

'Here,' he added, 'I wrote some of it down. Mary, where did I put all that stuff from our Mum's?' After a while, his wife appeared with a bundle of notes and letters done up in an elastic band.

'Here you see. They wrote it down for her. The evidence was only "anecdotal and coincidental". I'm not sure what the first means, but I take it that the second means it was just one of those things. Well, Mum then asked about why Harry had been put away, and they said they didn't know anything about that. Anyway, the upshot was they said they hoped she realised they had taken what she said seriously and had come down to tell her so, rather than just writing a letter, and they hoped she wouldn't think anything more about it.

'Now I was at sea at the time and Mum never did like telling her business around the place. But later she told me she'd thought about it a lot when they'd gone. One of the chaps had left his name and address from the Ministry, so she wrote again and said she still wasn't happy about it all and had they ever tried to find out why three people had died so near together like that. I believe, you see, they all died in different places, so it didn't make too much stir here.

'The next thing, Mum told me when I went to see her after all this – one of the men was back again and this time with a doctor. She said he was real nasty and gave her a terrible fright. He said that if she went on saying things like she was and making up stories, then she could end up where Harry Wharton was. He said Harry had had to be put away for his own good for telling stories that weren't true. He said that if she kept on, then he'd come down with another doctor and have her put in St Leonard's, and how would she like to end her days in a place like that? Mum told them I'd never let it happen, but they told her that they could do it anyway.

'I told her certainly I'd never let it happen. I admit, too, that I also said I thought she was making a fuss over nothing or at least nothing she could do anything about and that it was better she left well alone. It was past history and there was nothing to be done. She didn't need no compensation, I'd always see she was all right.

'When I left her she was not right at all, not herself, and I was going to go back and see her in a day or so. But then someone on another boat in our fleet had an accident and I had to go in his place, and while I was at sea she took the pills.'

'And you never brought any of this up at the inquest?'

'There didn't seem any point. It looked pretty daft in the light of day, you might say. It's true, old people do get bees in their bonnets, and if she'd spent a couple of hours up with old Harry, and he wasn't right in his mind about it, then I can see how she'd come to dwell on it. Mind you, I don't say I didn't think about it a bit at the time, but pondering over it wouldn't bring her back. I'm real sorry it ended like that for her, though. She should have had a bit more life ahead of her.'

Then, suspiciously, he asked, 'Here, you aren't going to start writing all this down for the papers, are you?'

Bill assured him they were not. He repeated that there had been 'stories' circulating about Shingle Street and they had merely been looking into past incidents.

'Seems an unlucky kind of place,' said Mike Fenn. 'Wasn't a young chap found dead on the beach there recently?'

'You can't blame them,' Bill said to Janet on their way back. 'They've all been caught up in something they can't understand, and none of them, except Harry and the old girl, Mrs Fenn, ever really tried to do anything about it. When the accident, whatever it was, happened, the boys running the place must have realised almost straight away, as soon as they heard that the whole team had been taken ill.

'So what do they do? Giggs and Burrows are whipped away, and to separate hospitals. Fenn dies almost immediately. Harry is ill and he's in hospital in yet another place. Burrows leaves a wife and a family of tiny children. She's an ordinary little woman, and it's all she can do to keep going for the sake of the kids. Giggs's wife is suspicious but is scared of sticking her neck out and making a fuss and doesn't know where to turn for help. None of these people knew each other very well outside work – I mean the wives and families weren't in and out of each other's houses all the time to know what was happening.

'Mrs Fenn doesn't feel happy either. But it takes years before she really decides to do anything about it and then she turns to the Whartons, only to find Mrs W is dead and Harry's safely put away where he can't embarrass anybody. By the time she tells her son, it's an old story, and anyway he's not around much; she's no real idea of what she's set going, but the powers-that-be are worried enough to send a couple of heavies down to frighten her off. And they do just that – they literally frighten her to death.'

'It's appalling. None of these people mattered at all, did they?'

'So far as I can see, the only thing that mattered was to ensure that whatever happened up there never got out. I think it had as much to do with covering up sheer incompetence as with keeping classified information from getting out.'

12.

After speaking to Colmore, Latimer got through to Chalmers in London and complained bitterly, first about the Special Branch sergeant's attitude and next about the fact that the Special Branch itself was concealing from him, a senior officer, its activities on his own patch.

Chalmers was unruffled. He understood that Detective-Sergeant Colmore was a very 'zealous' young man.

'Zealous! He's arrogant, cocksure, he's upset my own staff. He's upset local people, making totally unnecessary inquiries he had been specifically asked not to make and which we are sure have nothing to do with Spencer's death. He treats me as if I'm some junior clerk at the MoD. And you tell me he's zealous. I wish I had him directly under my control in my force for a few weeks, I'd make him zealous.'

'I can quite understand your annoyance, Chief Inspector,' Chalmers had replied smoothly. 'I'll see somebody has a word with the young man and the colleagues who are working with him.'

'And may I ask – yet once again – just what it is all about? You do realise, don't you, that other people may now be trying to discover what it was young Spencer was following up, and that by keeping the local police in the dark you could bring far worse trouble on yourselves. One of the people involved is a national newspaper reporter.'

'We understood he had been recalled.'

'He was, but he hasn't gone.'

'Look, Latimer,' said Chalmers. 'I realise it is very difficult for you. I promise that within the next forty-eight hours I shall come down myself and tell you what I can. In the meantime I would be grateful if you would do all you can to keep both the journalist, Baxter, and the lady – Mrs Simms, isn't it? – out of the affair. They can do no good now, but they could do considerable harm.'

And with that Latimer had to be content.

Before dropping Janet off at the library – nearly half an hour late, as she told him in some trepidation – Bill told her that he felt the time had come for them both to visit the old buildings at Shingle Street. Was she game to try that night? They would be less likely to be seen than if they went during the late evening, when there was always the chance of the odd night fisherman or a lad coming back from a disco in Stembridge.

'I think we should take your car,' he told her. 'I've got an uneasy feeling that someone might be keeping an eye out for mine. Can you get together a few bits and pieces – a claw hammer, if you have one, and a big torch? Good, and I'll bring some extra batteries. Wrap up warm and wear something dark – what's the matter?'

She'd begun to laugh. 'It's just ridiculous. Here we are, sitting side by side outside a public library in broad daylight, while you plan some kind of semi-espionage trip. I should at least be blonde, sultry and long-legged, while you should be smouldering and handsome with a sense of hardened steel under the surface – just like a paperback romance. Instead of which I'm an overweight mother of three, pushing early middle-age with a pedestrian job and . . .'

'And I'm a much more overweight, middle-aged, heavy-drinking hack with a failed marriage, who loathes any kind of violence. Should we run into trouble, fair damsel, do not look to me to save you by suddenly revealing that I hold a black belt in Judo or spend every Saturday studying karate. Let us hope there will be no need for any kind of heroics.'

As she settled back as unobtrusively as possible behind her desk in the library, she realised that she would actually miss him when he went back to London. He was amusing, he took her seriously and treated her as if she were intelligent. Besides, he had swept her along and encouraged her in a course of action she might have found too daunting to contemplate by herself. Right from the beginning, he had never made her feel that her intuitive reaction to Charlie's death had been foolish. That sense of something not quite right had been there to drive him on as well.

'How much do you think Charlie actually knew?' she had asked him on the way back from Yarmouth.

'Not very much, I suspect. He more or less stumbled on the accident story by chance and possibly got hold of some odds and ends from the *Bugle* files. He was bright enough to find Harry Wharton – we'd have been sunk without him. But he can't have taken the story any further or seen anybody else, or they would have told us. No, I think he saw Harry and then went up to Shingle Street on the Saturday night and found the place you told me about and broke in. What happened after that is still anybody's guess.'

Bill told her he would spend the afternoon working on the story so far, ring her about 6.30 p.m. to see that all was well, and then meet her at her house around 2 a.m. 'Will the children be all right?'

'We won't be gone all that long, surely? I'll leave their breakfast and a note to say I had to go out early and they're not to worry, just in case I'm not back. But I can't imagine that will happen. They're quite capable of getting themselves off to school and anyway, for goodness sake, I'm on duty from nine tomorrow morning!'

It was a young constable who discovered Baxter's car, while riding to work on his bicycle. He had passed through the village where Bill was now staying, seen a blue Escort parked at the back of a small private hotel, and gone to have a look. The number was right. There seemed to be nobody about and he tried the handle. The car wasn't even locked.

Its contents were not very exciting. There was a big, fat road-map book, several one-inch ordnance maps of Suffolk, the *Good Beer Guide*, an ancient raincoat, a heap of newspapers – the yellowing condition of the bottom ones suggesting that they had lain on the back seat for some considerable time – and a half-empty packet of cigarettes.

The glove compartment yielded some loose change, a number of grubby press releases for a variety of long-past events, and a piece of paper on which was written the name 'Fenn' and an address in Yarmouth. He copied this in case it might be worth following up and then continued on his way to police headquarters, where he duly made his report and asked what he should do next.

The sergeant told him to wait – Latimer would like to see him. 'Don't look so worried. He'll be pleased, I imagine. He's got a lady in with him at the moment.'

Frances Stimpson had looked dreadful when she had been shown in. Her face was grey under the carefully applied make-up, and her hair just rolled in a knot on top of her head. She appeared to have put on the nearest clothes to hand.

'Please, may I beg you, Inspector, to stop tormenting me?'

'Mrs Stimpson, I explained to your husband – nobody from here is pursuing you in any way. We wanted to find out if you knew anything that might help us with our inquiries into young Spencer's death. You told us first that you did not know him – understandable in the circumstances – and then frankly admitted that you had had an affair, which you had been trying to finish. You also made it plain to us that your husband was a difficult man.

'Had we been convinced that Spencer's death was connected with you in some way, then we would, of course, have had to dig deeper, no matter how painful it might have been for you. But we are pretty sure now that it had nothing whatsoever to do with you.'

'So why are your men still following me?'

'They are not my men. It appears they have been working on behalf of – of another branch of the police force.'

'From the Met? Is it anything to do with Charlie's involvement with that car gang?'

It seemed safer to let her think so.

'It could be. Anyway I have spoken to the superior of the detective-sergeant concerned and told him in the strongest terms that you are not to be bothered any further. I trust it will have an immediate result and I can only apologise and say, once again, that these actions have been taken without my knowledge.'

'I can only believe you, I suppose.' Suddenly she began to cry. The tears made rivers through the make-up. 'I don't think I can carry on much longer.'

'Once again, I'm sorry, Mrs Stimpson. Would you like a cup of tea? No, well you shouldn't have any further trouble. If you do, get in touch with me at once.'

She thanked him and left, bumping into the young constable on her way out. He wondered who she was and why she was so upset.

Latimer heard the constable's report and took the note he had made of the address. The name 'Fenn' meant nothing to him. He complimented the constable on his initiative and reluctantly telephoned Colmore to tell him where Baxter was staying.

'Good,' said Colmore. 'You checked he was there?'

'No. My constable had no such orders. He found his car – as you requested.'

'Jesus Christ – he could have gone by now.'

'I doubt it very much. I've already sent a car out to check, and my men have radioed back that Baxter's car is still exactly as my constable found it. Do you mind telling me just why it matters and why you want him so badly?'

'Yes, I do mind,' said Colmore and cut the chief inspector off.

13.

Latimer looked at the address on the piece of paper. 'Fenn' sounded like a place name. He could think of nowhere it fitted, but that in itself meant nothing, since the whole of East Anglia was full of tiny villages with odd names. He got out a detailed map of the area around Great Yarmouth. Drawing a twelve-mile radius, he found no trace of a village of that name within it.

A surname perhaps? The Yarmouth telephone directory yielded about twenty Fenns. Four were in Great Yarmouth, and the second of these had the same address as the one on the note. He was in luck. If the Fenns had not been on the telephone, it would have meant his slogging his way through the electoral roll.

He rang the number and a young woman answered the phone. Yes, she was Mrs Fenn. No, her husband wasn't there – he was back out to sea again, fishing. Would he be gone long? Several days, he was on the trawlers, not fishing for pleasure. But could she take a message?

With some hesitation he told her he was Chief Inspector Latimer, ringing from Stembridge police headquarters. Mrs Fenn became thoroughly alarmed. She didn't want to get involved with the police, she'd done nothing. She had had a trying couple of days.

Some people from the newspaper had already been that morning and talked to her husband before he had joined his boat.

'Was it a Mr Baxter – and a lady?' Latimer asked.

'I'm not too sure if that was the name. He was a tallish gentleman going a bit grey, and the lady was dark. They were working on some story, they said, and they wanted to hear all about my mother-in-law.'

'Your mother-in-law?' Latimer was incredulous. 'Whatever for?'

'Well, they seemed very interested to know about the time she died and that. But there was nothing funny like. The poor old girl committed suicide, took an overdose. I couldn't see why they needed to rake it up again. Poor old thing had gone a bit simple in her head, like some old people do. Kept saying she'd always known she hadn't had the truth about her old man's death – her old man died about fifteen years ago. My Mike's ever such an easygoing chap and his Mum's death quite cut him up – her going and doing it while he was at sea – and he thought there was no harm in going over the story again. In fact he said afterwards they'd made him think a bit. About his Dad.'

'Did he say what it made him think about . . .'

'His Dad's death. He was a plumber and died after he'd worked at some old laboratory or something but it hadn't nothing to do with his work. Leastways, we never thought it did. He just had a heart attack and died.'

'Mrs Fenn, do you know where your father-in-law had been working?'

'Funnily enough I do, sir. My husband told me before he left and it struck me because it was a funny name for a place, more like a road name.'

'Shingle Street?'

'That's right, sir. How did you know?'

She told Latimer that her mother-in-law's death had been duly reported in the *Bugle* at the time, and he thanked her. He tried to sort out in his mind what appeared to be a trail of ill-assorted deaths: first Spencer; then the death of a plumber fifteen years ago after a job which – by coincidence? – occurred after he had worked in 'some kind of a laboratory' in Shingle Street; and that one followed by the suicide of his widow. Three deaths, all linked by Shingle Street. And somewhere ahead of him, Baxter and Janet Simms were burrowing about. No wonder Colmore wanted to distract attention away from the real inquiry. It was obvious that there was a direct link in all this and that Spencer had somehow got on to it. It was time to tackle Chalmers again.

Chalmers, however, was not in his office. He had gone away for a couple of days, Latimer was told. No, they could not say precisely when he would be returning. He might ring in – could a message be left? Latimer left one, asking Chalmers to contact him urgently, day or night. Then he sent for a car and went into Ipswich.

At the *Bugle* offices they expressed some surprise when he said that he wanted to go through their files himself. 'I want a copy of anything you have connected with the suicide of a Mrs Eliza Fenn, about three years ago. And the inquest report.'

It was a hot day, and the sun beat down through the modern glass offices. He didn't envy anyone who had to work in this greenhouse atmosphere. Eventually a young woman arrived with some bound copies of the paper.

'I've marked what I think you want,' she said. 'If you need any more help, just ask me.'

He read and reread the reports until he had a headache, trying to establish the links. It was obvious that Eliza Fenn's death had been treated as that of an old lady who had become somewhat senile and was suffering from delusions, unspecified, but connected with, the death of her husband some years before. There was no doubt that she had taken an overdose of her prescription drug, since she had left a note to that effect, and even apologising for the trouble she would cause.

It was not an uncommon story. There was no suggestion of any mystery. Latimer could not see what else he could do immediately. Michael Fenn would be away for several days and therefore could not be questioned. Until he returned, there was nothing further to be discovered. He decided it would be a good idea for him to see Janet Simms and, this time, to be more interested in what she had to say – if she still wanted to say it.

He looked at his watch. It would be her children's suppertime. He thought he would leave it until a little later. He also decided that, whatever the outcome of his conversation with her might be, he would tell Chalmers straight what he knew so far and tell him with equal force that he would continue now with his own inquiries, since there appeared to be a direct link between the information being sought by Baxter and Mrs Simms and Spencer's death.

As he was driven back to Stembridge, he went back over it all again. Charles Spencer had told Janet Simms that he had been on the point of a scoop. Perhaps, after all, she hadn't told him all she knew. He had, he admitted to himself, been less than encouraging. She had then begun to look into it herself, and something must have happened between her first and second visits to him, for she had clearly taken the story further.

Baxter, also tipped off by Spencer, had arrived on the trail and, again following some unknown event, the two had got together, possibly after Colmore's first heavy-handed search of her property and attempt to frighten her off. The Special Branch would have a fairly good idea of what she was doing if she used her telephone to confide at all. He intensely disliked the idea of using taps without the authority of the Home Secretary and especially on people who were clearly not criminals.

For much of this time he had been concentrating on the Stimpson connection with Spencer. Had there been an obvious medical reason for Spencer's death, he would still be pursuing it. From what he now knew of Terence Stimpson's private life, any known lover of his wife would have had short shrift. Had the man known of his wife's sexual habits before he married her? She must have covered up her tracks very well. Then what? Probably she had become bored; then her husband's violent behaviour – even if it only happened occasionally – had given her a distaste for him, and the shopping trips to London to see old friends and go to the theatre had turned into something more. Had he ever had his wife followed? Possibly he had considered that beneath his dignity and she had been very careful not to do anything untoward in Suffolk. Latimer still felt distinctly uneasy about the situation.

So Simms and Baxter had started working together on some line that had taken them away somewhere, had annoyed Colmore, and also involved the family of a fisherman whose mother had committed suicide some three years ago and whose father had died after a visit to Shingle Street.

He was not a man given to fantasies, but at least two people had had distinctly ill luck following a visit to what, after all, was an innocuous enough place. He knew, vaguely, that there was still MoD land at the back of it, but there were thousands of acres of land on the coast, similarly tied up in MoD sites – stores, radar stations, dumps, the American bases. The MoD and the respective services concerned policed these themselves. They did not come within his term of reference, unless one of the men from either the British or American bases caused trouble outside and was arrested. It happened occasionally – usually driving offences or drunk and disorderly charges. Anyway, he would talk to Janet Simms again later on in the evening.

Baxter went down to get his maps out of the car. He was rooting about in the back seat, among the maps and debris, when he heard the car pull up alongside. He straightened up and, to his sinking dismay, saw four hefty young men get out. They came towards him.

'Can I help you?' he asked.

'Is this your vehicle?'

'Yes. Why?'

'And your name is William Baxter?'

'Indeed it is. And what's yours?'

'No need to be clever. My name is Colmore, Detective-Sergeant James Colmore, Special Branch, and I would like you to accompany me in order to answer a few questions.'

Bill noted the cropped fair head, the pasty skin and small blue eyes – funny how many unpleasant people had fanatical blue eyes, he thought, irrelevantly – a right cocky little bastard. This must have been the fellow who visited Janet. He sized him up and down and did not like what he saw.

'I've absolutely no intention of accompanying you anywhere. I've no proof you're who you say you are, and if you are, then you can ask me any questions you want to, right here.'

Wearily, Colmore pulled out his warrant card.

'All you people act like something on the TV – "Let's see your warrant card," ' he mimicked in a high-pitched voice. 'Satisfied?'

'No. Since you know who I am, you'll also know that I'm employed by the *Clarion*. I shall now go straight into the house and telephone them and tell them what has happened.'

'That'll be a bit difficult, won't it? You're not supposed to be here. Called off your story, aren't you? All they know is that you're taking a few days' leave and won't be in until next week. So if they don't hear from you for a little while, they won't think anything of it, will they? I wouldn't think your editor would be very sympathetic even if he was to know, seeing that you shouldn't be here. Now you're coming with us.'

'Look, we haven't yet reached the stage of a police state, however much people like you might wish we had. You can't just take me away to God knows where without even telling me what it's about. I'm not under arrest, am I, and if I were you'd have to charge me and let me contact my solicitor.'

'All right. We'll play it your way. William Baxter, I am arresting you under the Prevention of Terrorism Special Powers Act. This entitles us to hold you up to five days without further charges, and you will now accompany us to our headquarters.'

'You must be mad. What the hell are you trying to suggest? That I'm a member of the IRA? A Libyan hit-man on the run? Have a bit of common sense.'

'You've not shown much of it yourself, have you? Now get in the car and we'll ask the questions when we get where we're going.'

'And where's that?'

'RAF Bawdsey. We're using their facilities, though you don't need to know that.'

There was obviously nothing he could do. He did not think for one moment that he was genuinely suspected of terrorist activities. He had merely become an embarrassment and Colmore had used an all-embracing Act to get him out of the way. He would now be quite helpless and he wondered what Janet would think when it got to 6.30 and she received no telephone call.

'Look, can I just leave a message with the landlady here. I was meeting friends for dinner tonight.'

Colmore opened the door of the car. 'Just get in, sunshine.'

The landlady, looking out of her kitchen window, was surprised to see her new lodger climbing in the back of a large, black car with four other men. If it wasn't such a silly idea, she'd have thought it looked just like those thrillers on TV.

14.

Janet gave her children their tea, prised her son's earphones off until he finished his homework, and found herself obsessively watching the clock. By ten minutes to seven she had received no call and decided that she must ring Bill. Her friend Mark's fears of her telephone being tapped must surely be exaggerated.

A girl answered the phone.

'Can I speak to Mr Baxter, please?'

'Sorry,' said the girl, her voice just audible over the sound of thundering pop music. 'He's not here. He must be out.'

Her heart sank.

'Thanks, I'm sure he'll be back soon. I'll ring again in half an hour.'

The half-hour crept slowly by. She helped Robin with his English homework, found a miscellaneous collection of odd articles for Emma to take to handicraft class the next morning, and scrubbed Edward's football shorts – not the kind of activity indulged in by the average sleuth, she thought.

At half-past seven she rang again, and the same laconic voice replied that Mr Baxter had not returned.

'Didn't he leave any kind of message? Didn't he say when he would be back?'

The girl replied that she didn't know. 'He might have told me Mam but she never said nothing to me.' Mam was now at the Bingo down the Village Hall but she should be back about half-past eight

– 'that is if she don't go and have a cuppa tea with Nellie Briggs.'

At eight o'clock, when her bell rang, she flew to the door and flung it open, sure it would be Bill with some explanation for failing to ring. She was taken aback to find it was Latimer.

Her astonishment must have shown in her face.

'I'm sorry to bother you, Mrs Simms,' he said gently, 'but may I come in and have a word with you?'

She could hardly do other than ask him in. She showed him into her sitting-room. The two younger children were upstairs getting ready for bed, and Robin was in his own room, listening to his endless tapes.

Latimer saw a large, shabby, but pleasant room, the walls lined with books and, where there was space, a few framed prints. Janet's desk and typewriter were at one end, facing the long window through which he could see the mist beginning to curl along the river valley below.

'You have a pleasant view.'

'Yes, I'm just high up enough to be able to see the river. I'm very lucky.' She offered him a cup of coffee which he accepted. He was still staring out of the window when she returned with it. She asked him to sit down.

'Mrs Simms, twice recently you have come to me about your friend Charles Spencer, and on both occasions you told me you thought he had come across some kind of a story that he felt would be a scoop. You also mentioned that the story concerned the village of Shingle Street, north of here along the coast. I must admit I did not give you the attention you deserved. We were following up another lead that we considered more hopeful at the time. And I did not, I regret, take as seriously as I should have done your complaint about police officers searching your house.'

He was going to a great deal of trouble, she felt, to be accommodating. What did he want?

'From what I have heard, Mrs Simms, you have been making your own inquiries about Spencer – assisted I think by the journalist, Mr Baxter. Isn't that so?'

She nodded.

'Do you think you could tell me what you have been doing?'

85

His manner was so sympathetic that she felt at a loss.

'Do you deny that you've been pursuing inquiries on your own?'

'No. I can't very well. I imagine that I have been watched to some extent and I realised when Detective-Sergeant – Colmore, was it? – came back, on the evening after I telephoned you about my house search, that I was being monitored in some way.'

'You must feel that the police have not been helpful, and that we seemed unwilling or unable to follow up the information you tried to give us initially. All I can say is that it has been a very difficult situation – something which can arise when two branches of the police force find themselves working on the same case. I have now done all I can to try to prevent the situation continuing, and if you can pass on your information to me I promise to treat it in the strictest confidence.

'I know, for example, that you and Mr Baxter visited a Mr Michael Fenn at Great Yarmouth and that you were interested in the death of his father and the subsequent suicide of his mother and that his father's last job was at Shingle Street. I imagine, therefore, that you and Mr Baxter must have a lead of some kind, possibly given you by Spencer the night before he died.'

She did not know what to do. She could not understand why Bill had failed to contact her – he was usually so reliable. Supposing he had decided suddenly not to go through with it. She could scarcely blame him. If she told Latimer all she knew, would he, indeed, keep his counsel or pass it straight on to Colmore, after which nothing could be done? It was still essential, she felt, that she go back to Shingle Street that night, after which she could tell him the truth.

'I expect you'll find me annoying, but can you give me the night to work things out in my own mind? I promise you I'll come in and see you first thing in the morning – at nine, if somebody in your office wouldn't mind ringing the library to say I shall be late because I'm with you. I promise you then I'll tell you all I know.'

It was not what he had hoped, but it was a good deal better than nothing. Presumably she wanted to discuss the matter with Baxter before saying anything more.

He replaced his coffee cup, stood up and thanked her. 'For your own sake, Mrs Simms, please keep your appointment. No, this isn't any kind of threat from me at all, but you have got yourself into pretty deep waters and believe me, I actually do have your welfare at heart.'

'Funnily enough I do believe you,' she said, and showed him out.

As soon as he had gone, she rang Bill's number again, and this time 'Mam' was back from Bingo.

'No, Miss, Mr Baxter didn't leave no message. He just went off sudden-like this afternoon, about three o'clock. Not *his* car. In the other car, the black one with the four men in it. I didn't notice them arrive but then you get used to the sound of cars up our back lane and I just happened to be filling the kettle when I noticed this big black car, parked next to Mr Baxter's. There was a biggish bloke chatting with Mr Baxter and then they all got in the black car, Mr Baxter and all, and drove off. I thought it a bit funny he never said nothing to me. But I expect it'll be all right, Miss, he's left his car here and all his things.'

'Was the tallish man blond – about thirtyish – white-faced?'

'Couldn't see the colour of his face, my eyes aren't what they were, but he seemed to have fair hair, very short.'

She replaced the receiver, feeling sick. Should she, after all, go now and find Latimer and tell him the lot or should she go back to Shingle Street, one last time, and see finally if she could get to the bottom of the whole mess? At least she would see Latimer again in the morning and she would tell him about Baxter's disappearance. She was quite sure he had been taken away by Colmore and she felt equally sure that Latimer knew nothing about it prior to his visit.

Latimer checked back with police headquarters to see if there was any message from Chalmers. There wasn't. There was, however, a message for him to ring Colmore. He did so, with some reluctance. Colmore was at his most arrogant.

'While your lot were lazing around, we've picked up Baxter.'

'What are you holding him on?'

'Nothing really. He got stroppy, gave us all the usual stuff about his rights and a police state and ringing his newspaper, so I whipped him in under the PTA – or said I was.'

'What on earth for? Surely you can't imagine he's some kind of terrorist?'

'Hardly. But he's been mucking around with matters that come under the Official Secrets Act, and I want to know what he knows. The PTA's good enough for that, MoD, security matters, and so on.'

'I've already complained to your superiors about your consistently boorish behaviour and the lack of liaison between your branch and ourselves. May I tell you now that had you been more forthcoming to me, you would have made life easier for yourselves as well as us, and that had you contacted me before making this ridiculous arrest, I would have told you it was unnecessary. Mrs Simms is coming to see me first thing tomorrow morning and has promised willingly to pass on the information she has. What do you intend doing with Baxter?'

'Nothing much. We'll keep him here for twenty-four hours or so, find out what we can, frighten him off once and for all, and send him back to London with a flea in his ear.'

'Please, will you understand this. By hook or by crook I shall get hold of Chalmers at the MoD tomorrow. I shall tell him that unless I am put into the picture – properly and fully put into the picture – then I shall use the information I have myself in any way I think fit, regardless of your embarrassment. I have a resumed inquest coming up in a week with nothing resolved. Spencer's just as dead, and we're no further towards finding out what killed him. Now you've got some outraged journalist locked away who can make a real nuisance of himself on his release, and no doubt by the morning I shall have an equally furious Mrs Simms on my hands wanting him found. The net result of all this could be that neither you nor I shall ever know how much she has found out.'

Bill had been left alone for the first couple of hours. It gave him ample time to reflect. He assumed that if he ever got access to the telephone, his paper would get him out, but they would be far from pleased that he had ignored instructions and continued pegging away at a story he had been told to leave alone.

On the other hand, the fact that it had now got so far might, just might, prompt them to have the courage to use any story he came up with ultimately. He reviewed his past couple of years on the *Clarion*, and was discouraged.

He had taken the job because the paper enjoyed a reputation as a courageous campaigner. Maybe that had been the truth sometime in the past. But the kind of campaigns on which it now embarked hardly showed much courage. They ranged from appeals for kidney machines (with accompanying sob stories) to cleaning soft porn out of newsagents' shops. It was left to the uneconomic and overtly left weeklies and monthlies to tackle anything in the field of security.

He wondered what would happen if he returned and his editor said there was not a chance in hell of publishing his story. He might try to find an outlet elsewhere. That, presumably, would mean the sack, and the sack was no light thing. There were fewer and fewer jobs in his field. But for the first time he was prepared to consider the idea of making a stand.

After what seemed to be an inordinate wait, he was taken into an office where Colmore was sitting. After an acid exchange between the two men, Colmore said:

'Look, we're well aware of what you've been up to. Now you'd better tell us all about it.'

'If you know so much, then why ask me?'

'Please don't be clever. You were told by your paper to stop looking into Spencer's death. Why did you continue?'

'Because I wanted to know what happened.'

'For what reason?'

'Good God, man! Spencer was a human being. I knew him slightly. He was twenty-four years old, with his whole life in front of him. He tells me he's on to a good story and next thing he's dead. Jesus, man, that might be good enough for you, but it's certainly not good enough for me, and whether or not my paper wants a story, at the end of it all, I want to know what happened to him.'

Colmore tried a different tack.

'Why did you chase Harry Wharton up to Essex?'

'My friend Mrs Simms had visited him at the local mental hospital. She was surprised to hear he'd been moved and wanted to see the old boy again. What's wrong with that?'

'How did she find out he'd been moved?'

'The hospital told her.'

'I suppose you didn't ring them up claiming to be the DHSS and ask where he was?'

'Why should I?'

'I'm asking you.'

There was a pause. Then Colmore said, 'This isn't getting us anywhere. You know and I know that you have been poking your nose into matters of security, and I intend keeping you here until you've told me what you have discovered.'

Since this still did not provoke any response, Colmore said: 'Well, you can go back to your room for a bit and see how bored you get. In the meantime we'll be following up your lady friend.'

At eleven, Janet decided to contact her friend Mark once more. When she telephoned, she apologised again for ringing him late in the evening and asked him if there were any precautions that could be taken if someone suspected they might come into contact with any of the nerve agents he had described.

'You still pressing on? I wish to God you'd tell me what you're after. Well, of course, if it is known that there may be some danger, then any operative will wear full protective clothing, gas masks, the lot, possibly even breathing apparatus. Your average person just would not have the equipment, even if they suspected something was wrong. Rubber gloves and a mac won't do. The most minute area of exposed skin or tissue is large enough to absorb sufficient to kill you. I say,' he said suddenly, 'you did take my advice didn't you? You're not ringing from home?'

'I honestly did think that was taking things too far, Mark. I can't believe anyone would bother to listen in to me. There's no reason why they should.'

'I just hope you're right.' He sounded doubtful.

Half an hour later, Colmore was listening to the tape recording of Janet's evening calls, the increasingly frequent calls to Baxter's number – which told him nothing. They could genuinely have been because he had missed a dinner date, although it seemed a bit excessive. The conversation about the removal of Baxter by four men in a black car concerned him far more. She must now have a good idea of what had happened.

Then came the call to a Mark White in Lancaster, and that moved him to make a careful note. He played it through again and then sent for a Special Branch constable.

He handed him Janet's address, and looked at the clock. It was nearly eleven-thirty. 'I don't suppose this lady will be going anywhere at this time of night. But just in case, you'd better get down there and sit outside the house until morning. If she does make a move, follow her.'

15.

Janet went to bed and lay sleepless and uneasy until about half-past three, reckoning that this would leave her a couple of hours before it began to get light. She got up, dressed in thick dark slacks and an anorak, and left a note for the children, saying that she had to go out early and would Robin and Emma see that Edward had his breakfast and got off to school, if by any chance she wasn't back in time.

Prompted by some sense of caution, she had left her car parked a little way from the house. She packed a hammer, torch and a large screwdriver, along with a pair of rubber gloves, into a shopping bag and left her house by the back way. The back gate of the garden gave on to a narrow alleyway which divided her terrace of cottages from the terrace that backed on to it.

This manoeuvre was managed so successfully that the young constable in the unmarked parked car at the front of her house saw no sign of any activity. He looked at his watch. It was just after 3.30 a.m. The house he was watching was silent and dark. They must all be asleep. Cursing Colmore for sending him out on this job, he settled into the corner of his seat and dozed off.

As she drove out of Stembridge Janet found herself watching anxiously in the driving mirror for any sign of lights coming up behind. There were none. She decided to make the trip cross-country, using back lanes. Although it might take a little longer, she was far less likely to be noticed.

There was no sign of life at all when she got to Shingle Street. But all the same she reversed her car back along the lane and parked it in a field gateway a few hundred yards away from the wood where the compound was.

Once her eyes got used to the dark, she found she could see quite well and negotiated the path through the brambles and woodland without using the torch. The gap in the wire around the fencing was still there. She crawled underneath.

This time she went straight to the remaining hut. It looked exactly the same. She examined the pieces of wood nailed over the broken window and wished she were more practical, and certainly that Bill were with her. Gingerly she began to lever them off. It took a long time to loosen the first board without cracking it. The wood would have to be replaced so that no one would suspect she had tampered with it. Half an hour later she had succeeded in removing all three pieces. Then she shone her torch inside. The interior was disappointingly empty.

Annoyed that she could see nothing at all, she hoisted herself, with no small difficulty, up on to the sill and squeezed through the window, wishing not for the first time that she had the strength of will to stick rigidly to a diet.

Once inside, she shone her torch cautiously around. The hut was empty, except for one metal table in a corner, and it was very clean; remarkably, incredibly clean for an old disused building. It had been, very recently, scrubbed from top to bottom. The painted ceiling of plasterboard was spotless and whitened; the walls glistened. The paint on the window frames had been burned down to wood, and the glass on the inside had been polished. There was no dust, no cobwebs, nothing but a very clean, very empty space. She noticed that her feet had left faint, wet imprints on the floor and retraced her steps to the window, carefully wiping them away with her handkerchief. Presumably the dampness would soon dry. She shone her torch round once again but there seemed no point in wasting any more time. If there had ever been any clues in the hut, they were no longer there.

She struggled out of the window and began to put the wood back. Although she tapped the nails into the same holes, the noise sounded deafening. When she had finished, she stood and listened. It was quite silent. She picked up some soil from the ground and rubbed it into the scratches she had made on the wood and then crossed over to look at the bunkers again. Overgrown as they were, they were obviously there for a purpose. She imagined that behind the oiled doorlocks were more sophisticated devices, should any intruder actually manage to get a door open. She had no intention of trying. If there were still sinister substances to be found at Shingle Street, then this was obviously the place.

She looked at her watch. It was nearly five o'clock and she had better get well away before dawn. She had to admit defeat. It was while she was following the path to the roadway that she heard the sound of voices, and sought shelter in a ditch behind a thicket.

The voices and torchlight came towards the bunkers and the hut from the oppposite direction. There must, she realised, be another entrance, concealed, on the opposite side. It was a still, dark and silent night and the men's voices carried easily.

'I'm sure I heard some kind of a noise – like hammering.'

They tramped around, shining the torch and walking around the hut. She saw the torchlight glance off the boarded-up window and felt the cold sweat crawl on her skin. After a few seconds it flashed away again.

'Well, there doesn't seem to be anything here. Perhaps it was a woodpecker.'

'Funny time for a woodpecker.'

'What else do you suggest? Have a fag?'

She saw the light of the two cigarettes glow in the dark. In the dim light she saw that the men must be some kind of security guards.

'Quiet enough,' said one.

'Seems so.'

'Whatever do they keep in there?'

'In the hut? Nothing. At least nothing most of the time. About once a month they take a crate of stuff out of one of those bunkers, and it's taken away to be tested. To see if it's keeping OK and all that kind of thing. They usually put it in the hut first, and then a couple of chaps in special gear take it away in a van to some Ministry place in the south.'

'What is it?'

'Dunno. And if you've any sense you won't want to find out more than you're told. It's some kind of secret stuff.'

She was straining her ears as one of the men turned away, and she missed some of what he was saying.

'. . . some bit of trouble wasn't there? How often do we have to check this lot?'

'It used to be once a week but there was a spot of bother the other weekend, like you said, and now we have to come round every night. You'll get used to just doing what you're told.'

'What kind of trouble?'

'Questions, questions! I can't help you, nobody said anything. All I do know is that it seems a crate was left here over the weekend instead of being taken off straightaway. Two of our lads have been suspended and a whole lot of top brass came down from London and a load of chaps in fancy plastic suits spent hours cleaning the hut out, though it seemed clean enough to me already. There's nothing in there but an old metal table. Anyway they were in there with masks and special sprays and the lot.'

'You don't know why?'

'No. And I don't want to know. It'll all die down in a little while. This kind of thing always does. Come on, let's get back to base; I'm dying for a coffee.'

She saw the little light fall to the ground as he put out the cigarette.

'Shouldn't we look inside?'

'Can't see any point. Oh well, perhaps it would be better in the circumstances to be on the safe side.' He produced a bunch of keys from his pocket and unlocked the door. 'Here, shine your torch around here.'

She waited for what was bound to come. She saw the light flicker through the glass windows as it was shone around the walls and ceiling. Then:

'Hey, look here! Look at this! Someone's been wiping up marks from the floor.'

'Be careful now. We don't want to spoil the prints.'

The men disappeared inside and she crawled out of the ditch and began making her way as noiselessly as possible back to the roadway.

Back in the hut the senior security guard radioed his base and set off a full-scale alert. Colmore, who had long been in bed, was awakened with the news that somebody had been prowling around in Shingle Street and radioed immediately to the watching constable outside the cottage at Stembridge.

He jerked awake. No, he lied, he had not been asleep. He had seen and heard nothing. The house was in darkness just as it had been all night. And the car?

What car? There was no car parked outside either front or back, nor had there been all night. Furious, Colmore called police head-quarters for the number of Janet's car and told the constable to look for it. It was with sinking heart, some ten minutes later, that he radioed back he could not find any vehicle with that registration number anywhere on the streets or in the car parks of Stembridge. Colmore ordered a car and three men, scrambled into his clothes, and told the driver to get straight off down to Shingle Street.

Janet reached the roadway safely and, so far as she could see, without pursuit. She walked quietly back to the car. She was now more or less sure that she knew what had happened to Charlie. Poor, keen Charlie had chosen to break into the hut on possibly the only occasion when samples of whatever was stored in the bunkers had been left in it over a weekend. If the gas was kept in canisters, she reasoned, these would only need to be quite small. Presumably he had handled at least one of them and either found it damaged or, even more foolishly, had tried to see if he could take it away with him and damaged it himself.

She thought with real pity of what must have been a horrible death. His vision would have blurred and his breathing begun to fail, he would have vomited and, as his muscles contracted, possibly gone into convulsions, then died. Would he realise what had happened, she wondered, in those last few seconds of consciousness? But it still didn't explain how he came to be washed up on the beach thirty-six hours later. He surely couldn't have stumbled down to the shore in that condition and fallen in – and if he'd been alive when he fell in, there would have been water in his lungs.

Someone must have discovered what had happened and decided on a cover up. Presumably his body would have been still warm when it was found, and any sign of convulsions disguised. Then he could have been taken out to sea and dropped over the side of a boat. Whoever did it would have assumed that he might never be found or that, if he was, it would be on some other part of the coast. Besides, the odds were that by the time he was found – if ever – he would be totally unrecognisable, and no trace of what had killed him would remain.

She felt so tired. All she wanted now was to get home and go to bed for the few hours remaining before her appointment with Latimer. And how much should she tell him? She decided to think about it later.

Still walking as quietly as possible, she emerged on to the road and was relieved to see that it was still silent and in darkness. She walked up to her car and was bending over to unlock the door when she was grabbed from behind and a hand went over her mouth. She reacted instinctively and bit it hard. There was a grunt of pain and the hand jerked away. She turned round and saw Colmore, his eyes blazing with rage. Lifting his uninjured hand, he smacked her hard across the face, so hard that she fell over. Tears of rage and pain filled her eyes, and she could taste the salty blood trickling from the corner of her mouth. She was deeply shocked. She had never been hit in anger in her life.

'You fucking cow,' he yelled, 'get up on your feet, you fucking, interfering cow.'

Wiping her mouth, she did so.

'That's about your league,' she said, 'isn't it? Thumping women. That must take a hell of a lot of courage. What else do you do – shoot babies?'

She noted his driver looking on in some embarrassment.

'If you will poke your nose into what doesn't concern you and trespass on Ministry of Defence property, you can hardly whine when things go wrong, can you? Nobody asked you to come here, you did it all on your little own. If you and your boyfriend had kept out of it, you wouldn't be here now.'

'Mr Baxter isn't my boyfriend.'

'Mr Baxter isn't my boyfriend,' he repeated in a high falsetto. 'Not really? The other one was, too, wasn't he, your friend Charlie. Bit young for you, of course, but I suppose he made you feel better for it, a bit of young, rough stuff. What did the other one give you – more sophisticated pleasures? You'd hardly believe to look at you that you'd be fancied by one of them, let alone both. What did you do for it – pay them?'

'You foul-mouthed louse. I already have an appointment with Inspector Latimer tomorrow morning. I'll tell him everything I know, everything. *And* what's happened to me tonight.'

'You'll not be keeping any appointments, even with police inspectors. You're getting in here with me.'

She believed he was capable of anything. She wondered if she, too, would be found washed up on a lonely beach and felt a desperate concern for her children. She must have been crazy ever to have contemplated such a venture. She wasn't equipped for it. Her face was stiffening and beginning to swell. Then car lights came down the road and she felt weak with relief. Whoever it was, surely it would mean she would be seen? She wouldn't disappear without trace.

The car pulled up and a man in a neat suit got out.

'Detective-Sergeant Colmore?'

She began to weep. Obviously this was another car bringing reinforcements for Colmore.

'That's right.'

'And this is Mrs Simms?'

'Yes.'

'Well, Mrs Simms, I must ask you to come with me. Dear me, you appear to have hurt your face.' He looked from her to Colmore and, with a look of distaste, ran his eyes critically over Colmore who was sucking his bleeding left hand. 'There seem to have been a number of minor accidents,' he said drily. 'Mrs Simms, you have to come with me. These are orders direct from my Ministry,' he continued quickly, as Colmore seemed about to protest. 'Mr Chalmers himself is waiting to see Mrs Simms at Bawdsey Air Base.'

There was nothing Colmore could say.

'Do I have to go with you? I've already arranged to see Inspector Latimer in the morning.'

'I can't *make* you, if that's what you mean. But it might well be less unpleasant than leaving you to the tender mercies of the sergeant here. I'm sure he can find some reason for taking you away, and we can't be too sure what might happen to you then, can we, given the circumstances . . . I feel that the sooner this unpleasant business can be cleared up the better. I imagine you must be worrying about your children – they will be getting up fairly soon.'

Gratefully she got into his car, behind the driver. 'Take Mrs Simms's car back to Stembridge, will you?' the newcomer asked one of Colmore's men. 'We shall be returning her home – safely – later this morning.'

Bill had spent an uncomfortable night in the room allotted to him. He'd been given a cup of coffee late in the evening and nothing to eat. A blanket had been thrown in last thing, after he had insisted on being taken to the lavatory. He had finally fallen into an uneasy sleep from which he was shaken awake by Colmore.

'You'll be happy to know,' he told him with a glint of satisfaction, 'that your girlfriend is currently on her way to Bawdsey Air Base to meet a representative from the Ministry of Defence.'

'Why on earth . . . ?'

'She was found on the road coming out of the Ministry of Defence compound at Shingle Street early this morning. There had already been a report of a break-in of government property there.'

Bill noticed Colmore's left hand, still bleeding and with a clear set of teeth marks. He hoped they were Janet's.

'Is she all right?'

'Is there any reason she shouldn't be?' He followed Bill's eyes down to his hand. 'Stupid bitch. If she did get roughed up a bit she asked for it.'

'I suppose psychopaths like you are born not made . . .'

'Get up, you clever bastard, and clean yourself up. They'll be wanting you up there as well.'

'You'd better not hit me, had you? If you've already knocked her around it'll take some explaining in your situation, won't it? Not to mention what I'll do with it when I get out of here.'

'You'll do nothing.'

'Like to bet? Presumably I'll actually be seeing someone with common sense now, and if they have any, they'll let me go.'

He brushed himself down and felt the stubble on his jaw. 'On your way,' said Colmore, giving him a push. 'You've not heard the last of this, sunshine.'

Bill shrugged his hand away. 'And neither have you – sunshine,' he replied.

Up in Lancaster, a sleepy Mark White was woken by the persistent ringing of his front-door bell. Stumbling downstairs in his pyjamas, he opened it to find two strangers on the doorstep. His watch showed him that it was barely six o'clock.

'Dr Mark White?'

'That's right. What do you mean by waking us all up at this time?'

'We're Special Branch officers, Dr White, and we have a few questions to ask about a friend of yours – a Mrs Janet Simms – and just what she's been doing.'

'Janet. How the hell do I know – I haven't even seen her for a couple of years.'

'Maybe not – but you've been in touch, haven't you, very recently and more than once. We're interested to know why you have been advising her on the effects and nature of chemical warfare weapons.'

16.

In the back of the car, Janet strained to look at her watch. It showed nearly six o'clock. A greyish, damp dawn was stealing over the countryside, and for the first time since she had moved to the area she felt a sense of alienation from the place. Brought up in the safe, lush countryside of Warwickshire, she had spent her entire married life in central London. It had taken her some time to get used to the flat, marshy estuaries of East Anglia, but she had found her surroundings pleasant. Now the desolate stretches of marsh and shingle seemed bleak and inhospitable.

Her companion sat throughout the journey without uttering a word. The car wound along narrow lanes, often shadowed by overhanging trees, until the road opened out to an estuary. It was daylight by the time the car began running downhill towards the main gate of the base, and she shuddered slightly at the sudden sight of banks of missiles pointing east. She, like most other people living in the area, had grown accustomed to the bases – they had to, she thought, to stay sane. Bawdsey, like most of the others, was technically an RAF station but run, in fact, by the United States. She wondered if the Shingle Street bunkers came under the US as well. If so, that explained a lot.

The driver showed a pass to the sentry at the gate, the barrier was raised, and they were waved through. As the car pulled up, her companion said, 'I'm sorry we've had to do this, Mrs Simms. But you really had no business to be where you were, and Mr Chalmers preferred to use the base facilities rather than police headquarters.'

She did not reply. Her swollen face would make talking difficult and anyway she had nothing to say. She was shown through a doorway into a large building and along a corridor into a small office furnished with a desk and two chairs.

'I suppose you have some kind of toilet facilities – may I use them?' She was shown a door. Inside, she rinsed her face with cold water and, staring into a small mirror above the washbasin, saw her reflection, distorted by the swelling on one side of it. A mauvish bruise was already beginning to spread across her cheek. She wondered what had happened to Bill, and what her children would think when they got up and found she wasn't there. Had Bill told Colmore about their plan to go together to Shingle Street that night? Or was it genuinely bad luck that the guards had decided to check out the hut at that particular time? She wondered who Mr Chalmers was and what powers he might have to hold her.

Then she went back into the small office and sat on one of the hard, uncomfortable chairs. Her thoughts were interrupted by Chalmers himself. She saw a tall, thin man, who even at such an ungodly hour was clean-shaven and immaculately turned out. She wondered how he did it. He extended a hand. 'Mrs Simms?'

She nodded wearily.

'My name's Chalmers, Ministry of Defence. Smoke? No? Coffee then? Good.' He turned to the man who had shown her into the room. 'Rustle up a pot of coffee for us as quickly as possible, would you?'

He opened a file on the desk and began rifling through a pile of papers. Five minutes went slowly by before the coffee was brought.

'Milk? Sugar? Let me pour you a cup.' His eyes rested on her swollen face, thoughtfully. 'Has anybody seen to your injury?'

'No,' she managed stiffly.

'As soon as we've finished, I'll get one of the base nurses to do something about it.'

She took her cup of coffee and regarded him over its rim. 'Please don't bother.'

'I'm very sorry you had to be brought here like this, Mrs Simms – but you wouldn't listen to any advice, would you?'

She made no reply.

'Naturally we had to have you watched in the end.'

'Naturally.'

'Once you had been to the police and then started on what one might term your unofficial investigation, I'm afraid we had to take rather more interest. Then, of course, there was your visit to Mr Wharton and the telephone calls to Dr White in Lancaster.'

'You had my telephone tapped? That's what Mark warned me about and I didn't believe him.'

'An unfortunate necessity. Regrettable, but usual in these security matters. We don't always bother our colleagues at the Home Office.' He settled back in his chair and spread out the papers again. 'We've looked a little into your background, Mrs Simms. You're really quite a bright lady – no I don't mean that to be patronising. I understand you had a hand in uncovering a corruption case a year or two ago. Very commendable.

'To the business in hand. I expect you'll find this hard to believe, but I can assure you we had no idea ourselves at first what young Spencer was doing the night he died or why he was later washed up on the beach. It was a most unfortunate accident.'

'You're telling me it was an accident, are you?'

'Yes, Mrs Simms, an accident. What did you think?'

'At first I didn't know what to think. Then . . .' She hestitated.

'Mrs Simms, so long as you give me your undertaking not to return to Shingle Street, except on the beach if you so desire, I can promise you there will be no charges pressed against you – even though I would imagine, by testing your clothing in the forensic laboratories, it might well be possible to prove that you broke into the hut in the old Ministry of Defence station this evening. How those in charge could allow such carelessness twice is almost beyond belief.'

'I was very careful, but not careful enough apparently.'

'It should never have happened at all. However, you were saying about young Spencer . . .'

'At first I thought he had been done away with in some way – murdered, I suppose. That was before it began to look as if he might have been contaminated with some kind of nerve gas. Then I thought it more likely that it might have been an accident – only because it seemed a clumsy way of dealing with it,' she told him, gathering more confidence.

'Thank you,' he said drily.

'But I still couldn't understand how he came to be washed up in the sea. I assume he broke a window and got into your hut and he chose a weekend when, for some reason or another, some con-

102

tainers of one of your chemical compounds had been left out to be collected on the Monday morning.'

He said nothing but looked at her shrewdly.

'How much he knew about the effects of chemical weapons I've no idea. He did have a book hidden away behind the paperbacks in his flat.' From the surprise on his face she could see that this was news to him. 'Anyway,' she continued, 'I imagine he picked up one of the canisters and there was some kind of a leak. I think he managed, somehow, to drag himself out of the window and fell on the grass outside, scratching himself on the brambles before he – died.' She shuddered.

'Most unfortunate.'

'Is that all you can say?'

'Mrs Simms, it really was very unfortunate from everybody's point of view. Particularly that of the unhappy young man. But it was his fault, he had nobody to blame but himself. However, please continue.'

'I take it he was found by the guards, and they panicked. Perhaps they were supposed to keep watch all night and hadn't bothered, since nothing had ever happened before. I think they got the body into the sea somehow and then put out an alert. Your men came down and decontaminated the place, and it would all have remained a mystery except that Charlie's body turned up on the beach on Monday morning and triggered the whole thing off. Then you must have guessed.'

Chalmers got up and walked over to the window.

'That's a remarkably accurate description of what did happen. In fact the two guards carried the body down the beach. It was at least an hour before they discovered it and any possible contamination had dispersed, although they didn't know that. Then they put in a boat, rowed out to sea and threw it overboard. They didn't realise that the current set in such a way that with the onshore wind it would be brought in again so quickly. They had banked on the body turning up miles away, too deteriorated for any cause of death to be ascertained. They have, of course, been severely disciplined.

'As to your friend – can I repeat that it was a most unfortunate incident. He was quite plainly on Ministry of Defence property where he had no right to be. He then broke into a locked building and tampered with highly toxic material. Perhaps he even intended to steal a canister and take it away. Can you imagine what might have happened if he had, and there had been any kind of accident? There could have been any number of deaths. No, we can be thankful it was no worse. I'm afraid he brought his death on himself.'

She leaned over and poured out another cup of coffee.

'What would have happened if the men had reported finding the body? What would you have done then?'

'Let us say we would have found a – er – contingency plan had such an eventuality occurred.'

'What now?'

'I shall have a word with the local police and, with the maximum amount of co-operation from everybody, this should see the end of the matter. The inquest will be resumed and a verdict of accidental death will be recorded. It would hardly be in the interests of Mr Spencer's family for them to be told he had died breaking into government property. 'No,' he continued, as she started to speak, 'please don't think of the newspapers. Mr Baxter's editor is already aware that security does not allow this to be a subject for open discussion. The same would apply to any other newspaper.'

'I suppose it would prove embarrassing.'

'There is rather more to it than that, Mrs Simms. As you may have read through other – er – leaked information, the government is at present involved in delicate negotiations with the United States about the storing of their chemical weapons in this part of the country.'

'How appalling!'

'Appalling, maybe; necessary, yes. The American weapons would, however, be stored in their constituent parts to avoid any possibility of accident and would only become activated when combined. However, any story of this nature which emerged in the press would only arouse quite unnecessary public concern at a crucial time, when it is essential to the future of NATO that we allow the United States to store their weapons here. Our own store at Shingle Street consists only of a small stock of nerve gas left over from when we manufactured our own. We don't want the public to think there might be any possibility of any accidents.'

'But there already have been accidents, not just Charlie. You must know very well that he was following up what happened in one of the labs up there fifteen years ago. And you must know I know, since you've been watching my every move and have even mentioned my visit to Harry Wharton.'

'Ah yes, Mr Wharton. That was certainly, let us say, a sad mishap.'

'A mishap! My God, three people actually *died* after working there, through no fault of their own. They weren't breaking and entering like Charlie. And poor Harry's spent years in one mental hospital, and has now been taken away to another, all for speaking the truth. Not to mention Eliza Fenn who committed suicide after she'd been pressured by your colleagues. And all you can do is call it a mishap!'

'Hm – Mr Wharton, again most unfortunate. I know you don't like my use of these words. Far be it from me to criticise my predecessors but I agree that these things could have been dealt with more tactfully.'

'That is quite an understatement.'

'In fact I intend to have a word with my superiors to see what can be done for him. We couldn't call it compensation, of course, but we could say we had, after all, decided to give him an ex gratia payment as he had been working for a government department. Probably we could have him moved, perhaps to a small private home for the disabled nearer his home. Somewhere where he could be cared for pleasantly.'

'I would think that is the least you could do.'

'It might, though, in part depend on you.'

'On me? How?'

'On your now forgetting all about this whole business. No further investigations, no telephone calls to friends about chemical weapons. I'm afraid your friend Dr White must have been somewhat unnerved to be woken up by the Special Branch first thing this morning. Get back to your job and your hobbies. I understand you're interested in theatre – splendid, splendid! I always try to take my wife to Stratford at least once every season.'

She had a mad glimpse of him ushering his wife, a blue-rinsed, upper-class female, into the stalls at Stratford after finishing a relaxing day discussing the latest hideous weapon.

'Your friend Mr Baxter is next door, and when he and I have had a little chat he will, of course, be quite free to go back to London and resume his employment. The Special Branch will take no further action.'

'Mr Chalmers, what *did* happen at Shingle Street? Originally? In the war – what made everybody afraid of the place?'

'I'm afraid I'm unable to say anything at all about that. You must admit I've been extremely open and frank with you.'

'And tied me up so I can do nothing about it, if I want poor old Harry to have any kind of a life . . .'

'Mind you, Mrs Simms, you've been very perceptive. Perhaps you can tell me something. What made you so certain, so early on, there was something more to Spencer's death?'

'It didn't feel right. I have an intense dislike of things that don't feel right.'

'Well you certainly have a nose. Perhaps,' he said jokingly, as he showed her to the door, 'I could find you a job in government security, so you could work for the other side? After the appropriate security clearance, of course.'

'Which would be pretty difficult.'

'Which would, as you say, be difficult. Difficult, but not impossible.'

He led her through the corridor to the waiting car. As she got in she turned to him and said, 'It is a poison in the blood . . .'

'What?' he replied, somewhat startled. 'Nerve gas?'

'No. The whole bloody system. Your whole bloody system. Work with you? I'd rather work in the sewers – at least the work done there is honest.'

He stepped back and she was pleased to see his look of discomfort. Recollecting himself, he bowed slightly and turned away. Then he stepped back again.

'It won't be necessary for you to keep your appointment with Inspector Latimer now. I shall be seeing him myself at nine o'clock.'

Her children were already up when she reached home. It seemed like a scene from another life. 'Whatever have you done to your face, Mum?' inquired Emma. 'Yes, and where have you been?' echoed Robin.

'I'll tell you some of it some time. But not now.' She made toast and reassured them as well as she could, before seeing them off to school. She searched the back of her sideboard cupboard for a bottle of brandy left over from Christmas and drank a large glass, followed by several cups of tea. She could not face the library and wondered what the head librarian would say this time. At least she would not be having any more time off in the foreseeable future. Just before nine o'clock she rang to say she was ill. Irene answered the phone. 'A tummy bug? It must be the same thing Mr Thompson's got. He won't be in today either, so not to worry. It's pretty quiet. Do you think you'll be OK tomorrow?'

'Yes – yes I do. Everything will be back to normal.'

It would all be quite normal, except that Charlie's family would still be mourning the death of their son and would never know what happened to him. He would be buried and that would be that. Three other men were dead and buried and their secrets with them. Harry's improved life depended on her own silence. The waste had indeed filled the whole bloodstream, as well as having killed. In a little while she would recover her car from the police station and leave a message for Latimer that she was back at home, should he want to see her, but she didn't think he would. Both of them, in their different ways, had been equally washed by the tide of official secrecy. In retrospect she thought he had probably known less about what was happening than she had.

As she went to run a bath, the telephone began to ring.

17.

It was to be the second time in one day that Chalmers felt he had been regarded with contempt – this time by Latimer. The two men were sitting in his office, just after nine o'clock.

Latimer had been woken just after seven by Sergeant Chapman ringing from police headquarters. His wife had woken too, then put on her dressing gown and got up to make some tea. She heard his voice raised in anger. 'When? You've got him there? I'll get dressed and be right with you.'

'What's happened, dear?' she asked as she offered him the tea.

'It's Terence Stimpson. He's just walked into his local police station and told them he's blown his wife's head off with a shotgun.'

He strode furiously into police headquarters. He would have to put Janet Simms off and get straight up to the Stimpsons' house at Great Horton. He was greeted with the news that Chalmers would be arriving to see him at nine and that nothing – but nothing – must prevent the meeting.

'What happened?' he asked Chapman.

'Apparently at about seven-thirty this morning, Stimpson walked into his local police station, cool as you like, neatly dressed and shaved, and told them he'd killed his wife. The sergeant kept him there, whereupon he produced a neatly typed confession. So the sergeant sent a constable around to have a look.

'His wife was lying in the hall with half her head shot away, while the housekeeper, who'd been locked in her room, was banging away on her door trying to get out.'

'Put me through to the sergeant concerned.' He listened intently, asking one or two pertinent questions. Then he said, 'Look, I'm going to be held up by someone from the Ministry of Defence for about an hour. Get the police doctor up there immediately, and the photographer, and then leave everything until I arrive.'

He looked at Chapman bitterly. 'The confession is quite explicit.

After our own visit, the Stimpsons had two more from Colmore. Our response didn't satisfy Stimpson and he complained to Scotland Yard but at the same time he began to disbelieve his wife. The last straw came with an anonymous letter.'

'He's been around and on the bench long enough to know what to make of those.'

'Not this one. It was absolutely accurate as to dates and details – and it enclosed one of the letters we were holding from his wife. How the hell did Colmore get hold of that?'

Chapman looked miserable. 'He came in again the other day and asked to have another look at the Spencer file. I could hardly refuse, could I? His mob were supposd to be working on the same case, and you hadn't told me not to let him see any of the papers.'

'I'm not going to blame you for that. Anyway, Stimpson read it through and then tackled his wife directly and showed her the letter. She admitted it all – she could hardly do anything else – said it had all finished long ago, asked him to forgive her and so on. Stimpson's response was to walk out of the house. Two hours later he came back, after his housekeeper had gone to her room. Then he locked the door to make sure she couldn't get out, and quite calmly blew off his wife's head.'

'Good God.'

'He's sitting there now as cool as a cucumber without a trace of guilt.'

'What do you think he'll get?'

'A couple of years for manslaughter – no more. Respectable prominent citizen, blameless life, driven mad by jealousy of younger lover, etcetera, etcetera.'

'And all over Charlie Spencer.'

'And all over Charlie Spencer, as you say, ably assisted by the Special Branch. Yes, what is it?'

'There's a Mr Chalmers to see you,' said a young constable.

'Show him in – no, stay,' he said to Chapman who was about to leave. 'You've been involved in this from the start. I don't see why you shouldn't hear what he has to say.'

Chalmers was as well turned out as ever. He took the seat offered and looked inquiringly at Chapman. 'This is the sergeant who has assisted me on the Spencer case. He's staying to hear what you have to say.' Chalmers looked as if he were about to speak and then changed his mind. 'You must forgive us for being somewhat concerned with other things – a prominent local man, Terence Stimpson, has just shot and killed his wife.'

'How dreadful.'

'Dreadful, as you say. His wife, Frances, had been having an affair with Charlie Spencer. We'd known about it but stopped doing anything when I realised it could have had nothing to do with his death. But thanks to the pressure from your own department and the antics of the Special Branch, particularly Sergeant Colmore, and his attempts to draw attention away from the truth, we now have a murder case on our hands. When I put in my report about this, I shall ensure it is noted that I specifically warned Sergeant Colmore of what might be the result if he persisted in pestering the Stimpsons.'

'Perhaps you'd be so good as to tell me what happened.'

Latimer filled in the details succinctly. 'But Inspector, the anonymous letter could have been sent by anyone,' responded Chalmers.

'It could only have been sent by Colmore or one of your own dirty tricks department since only he, apart from Chapman and myself, had access to Spencer's file with Mrs Stimpson's letters to Spencer in it. That's a rare touch – to have actually sent one of the letters to Stimpson.' Then he added, 'Don't you ever find any difficulty in doing your job?'

'That's the second time this morning somebody's said something like that to me. I can only say no – no more than you find difficulty in doing yours. You above all people must know the necessity for tackling an unpleasant duty, whatever the consequences and however distasteful the methods which have to be used.'

'I've never been frightened of tackling unpleasant duties, as you call them. Equally I don't like seeing innocent people suffer. And now perhaps you'll tell me exactly what happened to Spencer and what this has all been about and make it as quick as you can – I have a corpse lying up the county with half its head blown off, and I have to sort it out.'

He listened in silence as Chalmers recounted what had happened to Spencer, and his subsequent meeting with Janet Simms. He also told the inspector about the fifteen-year-old accident and what had happened to those involved. Happily the incident now was completely finished – he could close the file on Spencer. A death by misadventure was all that would be required. Colmore and his Special Branch colleagues would be returning immediately to London. Judicious use of the Stimpson affair, linking it to Spencer, would finally quell any lingering doubts.

'So that's it, Inspector. You have nothing more to worry about.'

Latimer grimaced. 'What about you?'

'Oh we're all right. The Simms woman won't talk – the price of Wharton's freedom is her silence. Baxter won't be able to – nobody will dare print anything he might try to say. Nobody can actually connect Colmore directly with the Stimpsons. And as to Spencer – well, a rash young man, given to fantasising and a bit of a woman-iser – no great loss would you say?'

Latimer exploded after he had left the room. 'No great loss . . . maybe not. But what about all the others? Do you realise that there were *five* totally unnecessary deaths besides Spencer's? Three poor sods who died at Shingle Street because of inadequate safety precautions, an old frightened woman who committed suicide after being pressured to drop her compensation claim, and a married woman who fancied a bit on the side, and had her head blown off as a result. Oh, of course, and a harmless old man who's spent years in an asylum helping to keep the Ministry's feet clean. Give me good, wholesome police work any day of the week – this stuff stinks. Now let's go and see what's left of Frances Stimpson.'

It had been Bill on the telephone that morning to say he was all right and going back to London and would be in touch. Janet wondered. For a few days she bought the *Clarion* along with her usual paper, but nothing appeared. In fact, there was no story of any sort under his byline. She assumed that he had been well and truly silenced.

A week later she read the report of the resumed inquest on Charlie. A verdict of misadventure was returned. His body was taken back to London for burial and a family funeral. Next to that report was one of the magistrates' hearing committing Terence Stimpson to Crown Court charged with the murder of his wife, Frances. The placing of the stories did not escape her. Presumably this was the woman with whom he had been involved. In fact the story said that his wife had admitted to an affair with 'a young reporter'. The implication was obvious.

She wrote an apologetic letter to Mark, saying how very sorry she was to involve him in a very unpleasant business and promising to tell him all about it the next time she saw him. She was still waiting for a reply and she could hardly blame him if he felt pretty sore. He had, after all, done his best to warn her.

Latimer, to her surprise, had come round to see her at the end of the afternoon of what, in retrospect, seemed to be the longest day of her life. Like her, he looked strained and tired. He did not want to keep her, he said. He had merely called round to say that Mr Chalmers had fully informed him and to see if she was all right. His eyes took in the bruise on her face.

'A small memento from Sergeant Colmore. Mind you, I suppose he had more provocation than usual. I bit him.'

She saw a faint smile cross his face.

'I must admit I was happy to see the last of him myself.'

'Nasty as he was, at least it was overt. I found Mr Chalmers equally nasty in a much subtler way.'

His face showed nothing. 'I should get back and carry on with your own life if I were you, Mrs Simms. You've a pleasant home and plenty to do.'

'Plenty.'

Bill had returned to his office on the following Monday and told his news editor exactly what had happened to him. The only reaction he got was that the news editor told him he was a bloody fool to have involved himself, once he had been warned off. 'What did you think you were after?' he inquired sarcastically. 'Investigative Journalist of the Year?'

He was equally unhelpful when Bill offered him the draft of his story. 'Look – there's not a chance in hell of us using any of this.

112

You must know that. They've slapped a D-notice on it and that's that, finish, kaput. Now go away and get some work done. Somebody's been nobbling greyhounds and making a packet. Fred's got the details for you.'

Unsatisfied, Bill went to see his editor. Once again he laid out the facts of the case, finally spelling it out that at least half a dozen people had died as a result of the inept behaviour of the Ministry of Defence and that, however wrong it had been for Spencer to nose around a government establishment, his death had been caused by some slip in the way the chemicals had been handled and stored. On top of that, there had been the cover up over the previous accident, an accident in which those who lost their lives were in no way to blame. Surely to God, argued Bill, it was in the public good that such a story should be told? Especially as there were rumours that the government might take more stuff, this time from the United States, to be stored in the same area . . .

Exactly, the editor replied. And that was why he would be taking the advice of the Home Office and Ministry of Defence on this one. There was no point whatsoever in unnecessarily alarming the public. He then pointed out that Bill was fortunate still to have his job after his refusal to drop his investigation. It was only because of his past record that the incident would be overlooked. He had better be more careful in future.

'What,' said Bill, 'would happen if the story appeared elsewhere? In some less prestigious publication than a national newspaper, but if it appeared at all?'

'What other publications do is no concern of mine. I assume you mean one of the trendy lefty weeklies? Well, I can't stop them publishing anything they want to. But if a story should appear, even if it did not appear under your name and I could be pretty sure it originated from you, I'd fire you on the spot. Please believe me.'

'I do, I do,' said Bill, and went away to look into a case of corruption on the greyhound track.

His editor then sent a handwritten note to Chalmers, saying that that was the end of the matter.

Three weeks later Janet and Bill were facing each other across the table of a small Italian restaurant in Covent Garden.

'So you can imagine,' said Bill, 'how he reacted when the story appeared in *Time Out*. He came racing into editorial, roaring and screaming and waving a copy above his head. It was quite impressive.

'He had me in, of course, and said is this yours, and I said how do I know, all the stories in the front of that thing read the same. He said I know all that, but did you give them the information? I half thought of denying it and then I thought, what the hell . . . I'm absolutely fed up to the back teeth with the *Clarion*. So I said OK, what do you propose to do about it, and he sacked me. The union wanted to take it up but I said not to bother. He's had to pay me up to the end of my contract. So here you see Bill Baxter, freelance journalist.'

'I don't seem to bring people much luck, do I?' she smiled. 'Oh, apart from Harry.'

'How is he?'

'He's in a small home for disabled people just outside Stembridge. It's really very nice. I took him a copy of *Time Out* and his eyes lit up and he sent you his best wishes and fell on my neck like I really was his niece. It's a good job somebody feels like that about me – old Thompson in the library hardly speaks to me, the kids are livid because they know something was up and I didn't tell them, and I don't think my friend Mark will ever forgive me for involving him in all of it. I still don't know if my phone is tapped or how much notice they take of where I go. Latimer, the police inspector, has been pretty decent. I got the impression he was as sick in his own way as I was. Will it make any difference – all that we did?'

'I imagine the families of those people will get some kind of compensation, though it will hardly compensate the widows who've had to bring up kids on their own or poor old Mrs Fenn who was so frightened she killed herself. Apart from a brief report in the *Guardian*, nobody else dared touch it.'

'Are you disappointed? Couldn't we have been more effective?'

'What did you expect would happen? The Fifth Cavalry charging in and putting it all right? That's not how it goes. You just have to keep hoping that if you hack away and let a little light in here and there, eventually people will tumble to what's going on.'

He raised his glass. 'Here's to the future.'

She drank. 'What are you going to do?'

'I think I might try to start a small freelance press agency somewhere in the country. At least I'll be working for myself. Have you ever thought of changing jobs?'

'That's what Chalmers asked me.'

'Honestly? With your record?'

'He seemed to think I might be so useful on the other side of the fence that any – er – irregularities in my past conduct might be overlooked.'

'You accepted, of course.'

'Of course. Actually, I said it wasn't just nerve gas that was poisonous. It was the whole bloody system. No, I told him I'd rather work in a sewer.'

She looked at her watch. 'I'll have to go. It's been lovely but I must get the last train back or the babysitter, childminder or whatever you call her, will wonder whatever's happened, and my kids have been a bit edgy since my strange disappearance.'

'I'll pay the bill and get a cab and take you to the station.'

He took her to Liverpool Street and dropped her off.

'If you happen to be passing through Suffolk and feel like dropping in and letting me know what you are doing, please do. You never know, I might have another story for you . . .'

'I might just do that. Whatever next, I ask myself? Since you've managed to change my whole life and cut short my brilliant career, the mind boggles at what else you might have in store for me. Prison? MI5?'

'I trust,' she said, 'you're joking.'

The same afternoon, at Stembridge police headquarters, Latimer finally closed the papers on Charles Spencer, cross-referenced them with 'Stimpson' and had them filed away.

In his cool and tidy Whitehall office, Chalmers handed three cards to his secretary, the information to be put on computer. Baxter, William, and Simms, Janet, would go on to the list of those who are kept on loose surveillance for life or until they are considered too old to be of interest any longer.

'But what about this one, sir,' said the secretary, carefully

115

reading the third. 'Chief Inspector John Latimer – surely he's one of us?'

'He may be a senior police officer but I'm not at all sure he is one of "us" as you so quaintly put it. He is to be filed away just for future reference, no more, no surveillance.'

After the door closed behind her, he read carefully through the report he had received on the part Sergeant Colmore had played in the Spencer affair. He wrote 'advise no further promotion' across it, placed it in an envelope and had it returned by special messenger to the Home Office. Then he went home early. He was taking his wife to the theatre.

Author's note

There is still a mystery surrounding what happened in the hamlet of Shingle Street, in Suffolk, during the war, although I do not believe it had anything to do with this story. However, an accident, very similar to the one described here, did happen at the Ministry of Defence Chemical Warfare Research Station at Nancekuke in Cornwall in the mid-1960s. On that occasion several people died and an unsuccessful attempt was made to have the survivor sectioned under the Mental Health Act.

Manuel Vazquez Montalban

Murder in the Central Committee

'Thoroughly professional, wittily and pungently written puzzle by an awarded Spanish author... Not just clever, but with a specific gravity of intent, a density of stinks and flavours, a fresh angle on disillusionment.'

The Sunday Times

'...Montalban has also written on political theory (and cooking!) which may account for his exceptional grasp of the intricacies of left-wing political infighting, a subject no one has handled satisfactorily in fiction since Victor Serge... A must for left-watchers, but a tight and intelligent thriller too.'

Time Out

'...Montalban has managed to write both an excellent political novel and a gripping old-fashioned whodunit.'

The Times

'...The weary and knowing investigator, the rendering of political factionalism and knifemanship, and the insider's view of the Left in Spain make the mystery a rich brew...'

Tribune

'More Montalban please.'

City Limits

'...splendid flavours of life in Barcelona and Madrid, a memorable hero in Pepe and one of the most startling love scenes you'll ever come across.'

The Scotsman

0 86104 747 8   paperback   £3.50
0 86104 771 0   hardback   £7.95

Gordon DeMarco

October Heat

'...It's a zippy thirties-style and thirties-set thriller that would not have disgraced Hammett... Fast, slick and intelligent.'

The Times

'An overtly left-wing thriller in a genre largely monopolized by the ideological Right... . What is fresh is the viewpoint. It depicts a world in which the corruption stems not from individuals, but from the sort of society they have created and wish to preserve. Mr DeMarco makes his point without sacrificing his excitements in what must be the most innovative publishing experiment of the crime-story year.'

The Guardian

'...enjoyably and unashamedly in the Dashiell Hammett tradition, with the radical private eye uncovering a right-wing plot against Upton Sinclair's 1934 campaign for governor of California.'

The Bookseller

0 86104 744 3   paperback   £2.95
0 86104 770 2   hardback   £7.95

Nancy Milton

The China Option

'...Ms Milton does for Peking in 1984 what Cruz Smith did for Moscow in *Gorky Park* in 1982. Her perceptions of American, Chinese and Russian secret policies are all too plausible, the action is brisk and exciting, and the whole smell of another life on the opposite side of the earth flares the hair in your nostrils.'

New Statesman

'...The author, a teacher in Peking in the 1960s, clearly empathized with what she saw; scribes memorably about it; opens arenas of decency and otherness unlikely to find favour or comprehension with the CIA.'

The Sunday Times

'In fact it's pretty good... the geopolitical situation is not just convincing but downright alarming.'

The Guardian

'...her China is convincing and fascinating... The sophisticated political narrative is enhanced by the intelligent picture of the relationship between Anne Campbell, the investigating journalist, and a man from the US embassy.'

City Limits

0 86104 746 X   paperback   £3.50
0 86104 772 9   hardback   £8.95

Gillian Slovo

Morbid Symptoms

'What's genial... is the recognizable humour of
supermarkets, sprawling feminist mates,
horrendous blokes who feign understanding of
what women are about. She pertains... to today.'
The Sunday Times

'Lively and sharp-pointed...'   *Tribune*

'How refreshing to read a thriller in which neither
are the villains crazy reds nor the hero a macho
bully... And the sleuth is a socialist feminist.'
Elizabeth Wilson

0 86104 745 1   paperback   £2.95
0 86104 773 7   hardback   £6.95

Pluto books are available through your local bookshop. In case of difficulty contact Pluto to find out local stockists or to obtain catalogues/leaflets (telephone 01- 482 1973). If all else fails write to:

Pluto Press Limited
Freepost (no stamp required)
The Works
105A, Torriano Avenue
London NW5 1YP

To order, enclose a cheque/p.o. payable to Pluto Press to cover price of book, plus 50p per book for postage and packing (£2.50 maximum).